I Miss the Music

A fictional novel by:

Weldon Sipe

And

John Hadsell

With Contributions by:

J. B. Johns

And

Holly Fowler

Illustrations by: Robin Hall

Copyright © 2024 Weldon Sipe

All Rights Reserved.

No Part of this book may be produced, stored in a retrieval system, or transmitted by any means without the author's written permission.

ISBN: 979-8-218-45024-3 Paperback

ABOUT THE AUTHOR

My passion for storytelling began with screenwriting. I have completed over five scripts, one of which was optioned by a Paramount producer. Unfortunately, he passed away before the project began. Since then, I have transitioned to writing novels, debuting with 'Shadows ofa Christmas Eve.,

My writing draws deeply from my real-life experiences and observations, making 'I Miss the Music, a compelling and authentic memoir.

My career in the film industry began as a Location Scout and Manager in New Mexico. During my tenure, I worked with all major studios except Disney before relocating to Los Angeles. I,m particularly proud of my time developing and managing all the film related activity on the Newhall Ranch, which became the most iconic movie ranch in history. My efforts saw over fifteen permanent movie sets constructed, with up to nine companies filming on the ranch daily.

A trained actor since 1979, I,ve appeared in films like 'Up in The Cellar, (1970), 'The Man Who Fell to Earth, (1976), and 'Supercross the Movie, (1987). I also had roles in television movies, including 'Better Late Than Never, (1979) and 'The Great American Traffic Jam, (1980). More recently, I co-starred in the 2020 Lionsgate series 'Welcome to Flatch.,

ACKNOWLEDGEMENTS

John Hadsell was a professor at New Mexico State University. We became friends and writing partners on more than five screenplays. We wrote the first draft for this book as a screenplay in 1968, during the time many of the events portrayed were happening. It has been rewritten several times over the years to remain current with historical events. We eventually set the screenplay aside and went on to other projects. About five years ago I decided to write it as a novel. John passed away several years ago mentally unable to join me on this endeavor. His name remains on the cover as the co-author.

Once the first draft was completed, I elicited the help of J. B. Johns to edit the complex content, keeping a keen eye on the historical accuracy of events of the period. J. B. paid close attention to words with complex meanings, and references to ideas that shaped the present, by adding clarity of our memories of those times.

Holly Fowler, a very talented actress, made sure that there was continuity of each character, and between the characters, as I recalled the events, sometimes with great difficulty, and sometimes painfully, and weave them into the best explanation of what it was like back then, and telling you this story. Holly's contribution was essential to help me do that.

Robin Hall and I go back to when I was a location manager in the entertainment industry, and he was a design planner for a large land developer. He went on to work on all types of entertainment projects including theme parks, water parks, museums, and film sets. He was a perfect fit for illustrating a book because of his unique ability to connect readers with a story.

Life's Journey is not to arrive at the grave safely in a well-preserved body, but rather to skid in sideways, totally worn out, and shouting, "HOLY SHIT... WHAT A RIDE!"

Source unknown.

TABLE OF CONTENTS

INTRODUCTION

The title needs a little explanation. This will not be a story about music per se. It's just that the music of the times was such a reflection of the times.

We have added a whole new dimension to reading this novel by using QR Code technology. You can use your cellphone with QR Code reader software to listen to each song featured in this book. Use of QR Codes will take you quickly and directly to the audio file for your enjoyment.

LOOKING FOR AN ECHO – Kenny Vance and the Planotones

At Erasmus Hall High School, we used to harmonize
Me and Benny and Ira and two Italian guys
We were singing oldies, but they were newies then
And today when I play my own 45's, I remember when...

We'd practice in a subway, in a lobby or a hall

Crowded in a doorway, singing doo wops to the wall
And if we went to a party and they wouldn't let us sing
We'd lock ourselves in the bathroom, and nobody could get in

'Cause we were looking for an echo, an answer to our sound
A place to be in harmony
A place we almost found

And the girls would gather 'round us, and our heads would really swell
We'd sing songs by the Moonglows, the Harptones, and the Dells
And when we sang "Sincerely," we really sang it high
Even though it was falsetto, we almost reached the sky

We've sung a lot of changes since 1955
And a lot of bad arrangements we've tried to harmonize
Now we've turned into oldies, but we were newies then
And today when I play my own 45's, I remember when...

We were looking for an echo, an answer to our song
A place to be in harmony
A place we almost found

...

It is frustrating for me to roll a joint now that I am old. My hands shake uncontrollably at times. I don't know why. Once, I rolled nice, neat slim joints, thinner than a cigarette. Back then, much labor was connected with getting the seeds and stems out of the pot. If you didn't "clean" the weed, seeds would pop, and stems would ignite. Pot is legal and cheap here in Canada, and there's plenty of it. With pot's more sophisticated widespread marketing, I can afford to spill some when I'm trying to load the paper.

Rather than using a lighter, I always light my joints using wooden matches, which I also use to light my pipe tobacco. The even flame is better, and the aroma of the burning wood adds to the ambiance of smoking a pipe.

In sequence, I will tell you what happened to me when I was much younger. But first, I need to take a double toke, inhaling the second one more deeply than the first, holding it in as long as I can until I am on the verge of coughing. OK. That's better.

Now, life looks different as I recall the events that brought me to this time. As I recollect, there were times that I felt outside myself, watching it all happen. I think I can be more objective about the whole story now. I have to begin with relevant events when they started happening so you might empathize with my circumstances as they are now. If I were to tell you how I ended up here, you would probably be indifferent.

I was born an American. I grew up in a middle-class family having great memories of my childhood. I expected to live a happy and prosperous life and eventually die in America. And then, the '60s happened. In a nutshell, the '60s was an era of crisis. Because of the uncertainty and fear of being drafted into war, there was a waning of confidence. We knew something different and terrifying was happening to the country.

Young people today have no comprehensive understanding of that period in our history. I believe that's because most people my age don't talk much to the youth about that era. The trouble is that for each of us who lived through the '60s, there would be few parallel experiences to have a discussion that would not end in contention. So, most of today's young people just smile and comment about hippies and drugs. Yes, there were societal dropouts and a lot of drugs. But there was so much more beneath that superficial view.

Since the '60s are remembered differently by each of us, I will do my best to stick to just my story and not speak for others. For sure, the only general statement I can make about the '60s is that it was a time of confusing laws and contradicting social norms. But the one thing we all had in common was the music. Thus, the title, *I Miss the Music*. Rock and Roll was the overwhelming choice.

Whether a musician, college student, soldier, or draft resister, music was the communication thread that connected us. Soldiers heard the same music as their friends and family a world away. Awareness of war permeated the lyrics of the music.

Music was a reflection of all that was happening. We were connected through the music regardless of our political or social views. We were inspired by it. And we were motivated by the messages the songs contained.

In the 1950s, advanced communications, such as cell phones and the internet, did not exist for the masses. The dawn of rock and roll started with Doo Wop, an extension of Rhythm and Blues. The vocal group sound placed melody over rhythm, the song over the singer, and a blending of voices over individual style.

As anxiety over the number of inductees increased, music became crucial for the draftees. The war was part of daily life, even for those not serving in the military. The soldiers and those waiting to be drafted *needed* that music.

During those emotional times, music gave us a way to make sense of experiences that otherwise didn't seem logical.

That anxiety brought about a drug culture in the '60s. Love songs became psychedelic experiences on the dance floor, and music became a safe way to express our doubts, frustrations, and emotions.

I wouldn't be telling you my story if it weren't for a promise I made to my university professor, mentor, and writing partner for more than 40 years. John Hadsell died several years ago, not long after writing the first draft of this story with me. John felt strongly that truth is eventually lost through rewriting history, so I promised him I wouldn't let what really happened be rewritten.

With the help of my longtime friend and now co-author, J. B. Johns, this is the finished story as John Hadsell and I imagined it to be. J.B. lived through the '60s, too, and has added great clarity through her memories of those times, which are still very vivid for both of us.

Chapter 1

My story is not about any president or military general from that time because, back then, none of us gave a damn what they said. My story centers on the military draft. If some of you young folks don,t know about the draft, it gives our government the right to snatch young men from their families under penalty of imprisonment if they do not cooperate.

The government gave them uniforms and guns and sent them off to die in some political war or conflict, justified or not. As the historian Howard Zinn reminds us, 'We were raised to understand this as nothing short of being kidnapped. But our government never referred to it as kidnapping. They called it, 'Selective Service.,

Chapter 2
HURRY UP AND WAIT

About two weeks before my eighteenth birthday, I received a notice from the draft board that I had to have an army physical as required by Pennsylvania law. So, at 4 a.m. I drove to the designated parking lot of the local armory, where others were solemnly wandering around, looking anxious, confused, and generally resentful of being there. Two men in military uniform stood together beside a bus with clipboards. The mood was very solemn as one of the military men began calling out names.

"When you hear your name called, get your ass on the bus and take a seat," the short, barrel-chested one with a receding hairline bellowed out. "Jeffers, John Jeffers," he yelled louder.

I had hoped that his tone was not indicative of what the day was going to be like, but that was soon dashed when no one headed for the bus by that name. "Jeffers," he blared out angrily. A tall thin guy enjoying a cigarette in the back raised his arm. "Here," he spoke up, barely audible.

"Well, you recognized your name. That's a relief. If it's quite alright with you, would you please get on the bus!" shouted the soldier in a sarcastic tone.

Jeffers finger-flipped his cigarette butt onto the grassy area next to the gravel parking lot, then slowly proceeded through the group to the bus. Just before boarding, the soldier stopped him. "Say, buddy, can you spare one of those cigarettes for a pal?"

"Sure, Sir." He pulled the pack from his shirt pocket, and the officer quickly snatched it from his hand, threw it on the ground, and stomped it flat.

"Let's get a few things straight right now. I ain't your buddy. Whatever is important to me is your only, and I mean your only, reason for living. You got that?"

"Yes, Sir."

"And that's another thing," barked the soldier. "Don't address me as Sir. See these stripes?"

Jeffers acknowledged he did with a nod. "These stripes mean I am a Sergeant." "Yes, Sir...I mean, Sergeant."

"Do you have any stripes on you, Jeffers?" "Well, no, Sergeant."

"That's because you are just a dumbass warthog."

The bus trip wasn't anything much to recall. There wasn't a lot of talking, maybe some low-key chitchat. I recognized several others as fellow high school students, but we didn't speak. Others, whom I didn't recognize, seemed older.

Chapter 3
THE NAKED TRUTH

We could choose not to go into the military if we really wanted to; there was no massive draft during the early '60s. Actually, there was some draft, but the list of occupational exemptions and deferments was long enough that almost anyone could choose to do anything that would defer being drafted. There were student deferments and exemptions for being married, and ministerial vocations were exempt. Occupation exemptions deemed essential included agriculture, medical care, or being employed in the defense industry.

The following events of the Army physical are most clear in my memory. Other memories connecting them are fuzzier.

I-FEEL-LIKE-I'M-FIXIN'-TO-DIE RAG - Country Joe & The Fish

Gimme an F…
Gimme a U…
Gimme a C…
Gimme a K…
What's that spell?
What's that spell?
What's that spell?
What's that spell?
What's that spell?
Yeah, c'mon on all you big strong men
Uncle Sam needs your help again

He's got himself in a terrible jam
Way down yonder in Vietnam
So put down your books and pick up a gun
We're gonna have a whole lot of fun
And it's 1, 2, 3, what're we fighting for?
Don't ask me, I don't give a damn
Next stop is Vietnam
And it's 5, 6, 7, open up the pearly gates
Well there ain't no time to wonder why
Whoopee! we're all gonna die

...

About three busloads of us had formed a disorganized but peaceful group in the gym that soon became tense when a military person began yelling. I presumed it was their nature to always be bellowing. Almost as soon as we were exposed to them, we realized they were unhappy and resigned to set procedures. Within a very short time, their bitter attitude rubbed off on us, and we just wanted to go home.

I do remember quite vividly being naked except for some paper shoes and standing amid more than 200 other nude men in this large gymnasium. They were making us get down to the basics, you might say, to the naked truth, and prove we were physically and mentally all there.

Some guys looked worried, some looked hungover, and some looked like restless sheep. I was feeling just plain numb, but I cooperated. Most of us were only there to satisfy the law. Hopefully, by showing up, we would not aggravate our local draft boards into pulling up our draft cards any time soon.

"All right, gentlemen! Act your age!" a sergeant with a "Jenkins" name tag snapped. "All of you out of diapers, right? Then let's see if we can form a line, shall we?"

A moment later, the sergeant was joined by another one with "Balasko" on his name tag. When they talked to one another, it was like they weren't supposed to converse. A conversation between two soldiers is usually carried on without eye contact, and the muted words come from the corners of their mouths.

"New orders to step it up," murmured Balasko. "They need more meat."

"What the hell is going on?" asked Jenkins.

"A build-up, it looks like," replied Balasko shrugging his shoulders with a what-the-fuck attitude.

Little did Balasko know, he was more than right. The demand for draftees was about to explode.

Gradually we all began to form a haphazard line. Some were still milling about, which didn't please Jenkins. Then we were joined by another group of guys who seemed much more confused than us.

"Hey, you gentlemen," whined Jenkins holding back his anger, "Come join us, won't you please? Your country needs you. Don't ask me why they want dumb warthogs like you, but they do." He waited impatiently, arms crossed.

I stepped into the long line of naked males. To my dismay, Willie, my soon-to-be brother-in-law, stepped into place beside me. He arrived with the group that had just joined us.

What an asshole! Willie was kind-da-like one of those Italian dumbass, fat gangsters you see in movies; overly confident, overly everything. Likable, maybe, but as a poisonous pet snake, never loveable. I was there because the law said I had to be, and I was afraid not to be. He was there because he eagerly enlisted, and I was hoping to avoid him.

"You still sneaking around with my sister?" probed Willie.

"I don't have to sneak, Willie," I snapped.

"Look, Wendel Sippie, don't get your balls in an uproar. You don't exactly fit the family candidate profile if you get my drift." He always referred to me as Wendel Sippie to aggravate me, even though my name was Weldon Sipe.

I retorted, "Ginny knows what she wants. She can decide for herself."

Willie always tried to take control of the conversation. If he couldn't, he made sure to get the last word in.

"Let me put it this way, my little gumba, unless you want to work in the family road construction business, you better back off."

"Why'd you sign up, Willie?" I asked, "This can't be part of your family's business plan."

"National Guard. I'll only be a weekend warrior while working the business and guarding the country."

Apparently, Sergeant Jenkins had been patient long enough. He sarcastically asked, "Can't you retards form a straight line? Pretty please."

Finally, he burst out with anger. "Get those shiny asses in a line right now. Step it up!"

The sergeant paced for several minutes. Soon he began ranting and raving.

"Maybe some of you are thinkin' Uncle Sam is acting like a big bully, uh? All Right! Well, maybe that's just what we need, a big goddam bully! The bigger, the better! Them commies is too goddam smart-ass, and them chink commies is just waiting to spread out and take over. We gotta save the world for democracy, our democracy! We gotta show 'em we're the biggest bully. Do you dumbasses get it? Cause if you don't, you're nothing but traitors to democracy, our democracy, and you should go on out and eat grass like the dumbass warthogs you are."

"I like this guy," remarked Willie. "He speaks my lingo."

A skinny young medical doctor with a clipboard under his arm joined the sergeant. He was dressed in an oversized white tattered uniform, and it was apparent that it was on loan to him. The doctor whispered something to Jenkins and handed him a letter that brought him back to sanity from his tantrum.

"Giles, James Giles," he hollered out.

Giles hesitantly raised his hand and was extremely embarrassed by being called out in front of the whole group.

Jenkins stomped over to Giles, held the letter up to his face, and queried, "You brought in this letter from your physician that says you have a heart murmur?"

"Let me hear this murmur," said Jenkins putting his ear on Giles' chest. "I don't hear a murmur, do you, Doc?"

Even though the doctor had a stethoscope around his neck, he did precisely the same as Jenkins and put his ear on Giles' chest. Only two seconds passed, and the doctor confirmed with a nod, indicating no murmur.

Jenkins held the letter up to be visible to the rest of us, then ripped it up.

"Well, your doctor must have confused you with someone else," snarled Jenkins.

"All right, when I tell you, everybody bend over, look straight ahead, and spread your cheeks," barked Jenkins.

All of us bent over except for one person.

"I can't bend over," spoke a timid-voiced male.

"Who said that?"

"I did," said the young man.

"What do you mean you can't? Only a pussy warthog that isn't man enough to be in this Army would say I can't."

"My back is practically all metal wire," said the young man. "If I bend over, it will take you and two others to straighten me up."

"We'll see about that. Now, bend over,"Jenkins shouted forcefully.

The young man bent over.

Then yelling again, "Okay, the rest of you bend over, spread um, and remain in that position until you have been examined by the Doc."

He turned to the doctor. "Make it quick, Doc. Some of these assholes got to be in South Carolina by morning."

Willie, taking all this in stride, said, "Watch this!"

Quickly he bent over and spread the cheeks on his face with his index fingers. I could feel my face flushing with fear just being next to him and thinking about the likely retaliation he would get.

The Doc walked fast, almost running down the row of men. He slapped each guy's ass while quickly glancing at their cracks.

He hesitated when he came to Willie and looked to the sergeant, who immediately came storming toward Willie. The sergeant didn't say anything at first, and he just stood there with his hands on his hips, waiting to see if Willie would buckle under his stare. But Willie didn't. He just stayed bent over.

"What kind of a doctor do you think he is?" barked the sergeant. "You think he is a dentist?"

This was humorous, and many couldn't hold back a chuckle. "When we work on your teeth at camp, I'll make sure it's through your asshole!"

Some responded with groans of pain, just imagining it. Willie decided to quickly grab his ass cheeks and spread them. The sergeant looked at the doctor with a smirking grin.

I still remember the look of resignation Willie had on his face when he realized he wasn't going to win anything by pulling stunts. Still, the one thing I admired about him was his willingness to challenge authority.

Even in high school, he would challenge the teachers, like the shop teacher. He built a gun rack to hold a tommie gun instead of a rifle.

The fact that he even showed up for this physical was surprising. He had no taste for being a career soldier. In fact, he had no inclination to be in the military at all. He planned to avoid Vietnam by enlisting in the National Guard and yet get credit for serving his time with all the benefits and pageantry that came with it. For someone that was a dumb shit from the Bronx, he was apparently smart this time.

We were then called by name and split into two groups. As we were leaving, there was a commotion in the line as Jenkins and the doctor struggled to get the guy with the metal back to stand upright. Finally, being joined by another staff member, Jenkins held the guy under the arms. The other two pulled on separate legs.

Willie and I were separated. It didn't take me long to figure out that his group was all the enlistees. This was their callback, and they weren't going home that night! For them, this was the once-over to make sure they were fit to die for our country or whatever the government had gotten itself into, like the daily news of the Vietnam conflict, an undeclared war with no end in sight.

My group was then separated into smaller groups for this progressive physical. Each group was directed to a particular partitioned cubicle for a specific part of the examination.

Walking from cubicle to cubicle was an experience of humility. Female nurses walked freely through the gymnasium delivering supplies and records to the medical corpsmen at the various makeshift stations. Since the men were only wearing paper shoes, they were having fun embarrassing us and occasionally giggling.

They made audible comments about the size of a penis or physique. The only way to protect one's modesty was to cover your penis with your hands, and I perceived, as well as others, that would make you out to be a pussy. So, it was best to stay in groups to hide behind other bodies or just show it like a man, even if you risked being teased because there wasn't much there. I was average, so I opted to show it as it was.

The exam stations were equipped for checking sight, hearing, muscle coordination, blood pressure, and other things like blood and urine samples. Some inductees were uneasy about giving blood and urine samples.

We were given small, numbered paper cups to hold our urine samples. The cups were too small, so you can imagine the spillage from the overflowing cups onto the floor under the wall of urinals. Everybody tried not to get their paper shoes wet by assuming the most unusual stances at the urinals, but they weren't often successful. The samples were collected a few at a time through a small in-the-wall medicine cabinet that could be opened from the other room. An attendant on the other side of the cabinet asked our name when he called out the number on the cup, and he wrote our name on a clipboard paper list next to a number on the cup.

A few guys couldn't muster up a sample on demand, probably due to the overcrowded and embarrassing circumstances. Others helped them out by pouring some into their cups. With all this extracurricular urine activity, it was impossible to avoid all the puddles. So many of us spent the rest ofthe day walking around in wet paper shoes.

It was on to the hearing test, where I was told to sit alongside three other guys in one of four folding metal chairs. We were seated in a row in front of a table with testing equipment operated by another military doctor. I still remember how it felt when my nuts shriveled when they met the cold metal surface ofthe chair. The doctor had headphones on that were plugged into an equipment console. I could tell by his blunt words and sharp mannerisms that he didn't want to be there, and he was somewhat apprehensive about the equipment and the testing procedures. He listened through the headphones as he set up the dials for testing. Then he removed the headphones from his head and placed them on the head of the young man closest to him.

I just sat there observing. It's difficult to know much about others around you when everyone is nude. The seemingly only perceived difference was the size of our dicks. But somehow, I determined the first guy being tested was a country boy. The haircut he had was one of those bowl cuts that poorer kids got when they were little. City kids got bowl cuts too sometimes, but when they finally became concerned about their appearance and became interested in girls, going to the town barber with dad was the first step to growing up. Mothers continued to give haircuts to their country kids well into middle school, sometimes into high school. This recruit still had a bowl cut, appeared earthy, and had a sunburned neck, forearms, and hands. He didn't seem to care that he had a front tooth missing and whistled when he talked. He was antsy and seemed generally confused about everything.

"Just signify by nodding your head yes or no when you hear the tone," the doctor said to the farm boy.

The doctor didn't realize that the wires to the headphones were faulty. When he removed them from his own head and placed them on the farm boy's head, the wires shorted, and the signal went silent. The farm boy was to give him a nod, yes or no, when he heard the signal.

The farm boy nodded no.

Figuring that the farm boy might have a hearing problem, the doctor slightly turned up the signal dials and nodded to him to signal that he could or couldn't hear the signal.

Again, the farm boy nodded that he could not.

Annoyed, the doctor turned the right and left knobs up a little more.

Again, the farm boy nodded no.

Peeved, the doctor yanked the headphones off the farm boy's head and put them back on his head to see if they were working. Of course, as he did, the unseen wires sparked and reconnected.

He heard the signal but fiddled with the knobs a little to ensure the volume was still adjustable. They seemed to be working properly. I could see that the doctor was judging the farm boy to be a dumb shit, and he placed the headphones back on the farm boy's head roughly. Of course, when he did so, the wires shorted out again!

Figuring that the farm boy probably had a hearing problem, the doctor turned up the dials slightly and signified to the boy to nod yes or no. Again, the farm boy nodded no, which totally angered the doctor, who abruptly turned the knobs up to the max.

"Do you hear that?" the doctor mouthed. Again, the farm boy nodded no.

We were all watching intently as to how this would play out. Several guys were already chuckling while I was holding my laughter back.

The doctor lunged for the headphones and slammed them on his head without turning down the knobs. The wires reconnected, sending the signal at full volume to the doctor's ears.

He stood up suddenly and screamed loudly, "God dammit," which was heard throughout the gymnasium.

Suddenly, all got deadly quiet. In a second, the noisy activity resumed as quickly as it had gotten quiet. The doctor, still holding his ears, dismissed us without bothering to examine the rest of us.

"Get your asses out," he said, resigned to failure. He faltered. "You all passed. Get the fuck out".

The last station turned out to be a classroom. We were administered an intelligence test. Naively, I presumed that high test results would be beneficial. I did not realize the smarter path was to intentionally perform poorly. The others around me had undoubtedly figured that out and were haphazardly answering the questions. Some had chosen a column and filled all the same spaces by making a single straight line down the page. Some were even doodling. I, being stupid about what was happening, took my test seriously.

Two corpsmen observed us taking the test. They walked up and down the aisles. I thought they were making sure there was no cheating, but I was wrong. They were looking over our shoulders to spot the serious test takers. Anyone who was feverishly taking the test was of interest to them as a potential inductee. It didn't take long for them to zero in on me.

"Looks like we got a live one there," I could hear one corpsman say to the other.

"Recruit or draftee?" asked the other.

The corpsman checked his clipboard. "Neither. Eighteenth birthday."

"Go to work on him anyway. Maybe he'll change his mind."

I AIN'T NO FORTUNATE ONE - Creedence Clearwater Revival

… Some folks are born made to wave the flag
Hoo, they're red, white and blue
And when the band plays "Hail to the chief"
Ooh, they point the cannon at you, Lord
… It ain't me, it ain't me

I ain't no senator's son, son
It ain't me, it ain't me
I ain't no furtunate one, no

… Some folks are born silver spoon in hand

Lord, don't they help themselves, Lord?
But when the taxman come to the door
Lord, the house lookin' like a rummage sale, yeah
… It ain't me, it ain't me

I ain't no millionaire's son, no, no
It ain't me, it ain't me
I ain't no fortunate one, no

… Yeah-yeah, some folks inherit star-spangled eyes
Hoo, they send you down to war, Lord
And when you ask 'em, "How much should we give?"
Hoo, they only answer, "More, more, more, more"
… It ain't me, it ain't me

I ain't no military son, son, Lord
It ain't me, it ain't me
I ain't no fortunate one, one

...

The rest of the day was uneventful until we were dismissed and began to get on the bus. The inductees were herded into a separate group. I stood and watched as a corpsman told them to raise their right hands and repeat the oath of allegiance to the military. Willie was among them. Some raised their hands. Some didn't. Some randomly did so. Willie didn't raise his. Most didn't give a damn. The corpsman purposely did not look up from his clipboard.

Then the inductees began boarding the bus for basic training in South Carolina. Willie looked back at me with the strangest look; the best description was that he looked pathetic.

Just then, the corpsman who proctored the intelligence test came to me, and I knew he wanted to sell me something.

"Happy birthday, kid," he said.

I had no interest but to get on the bus home with the other eighteen-year-olds. He reminded me of a vacuum cleaner salesman.

"How does it feel to make your own decisions now?" "OK," I replied.

"You sure you don't want to join your friend? You can get on that bus right now, whaddya say? You'll be in uniform tomorrow morning, kicking some ass for Uncle Sam."

"I don't think so," I retorted.

"Sure now? I can fix it."

The last of the inductees, including Willie, were now on the bus. I became instantly irritated with the corpsman.

"What's my name?"

"What?" he muttered.

"My name," I repeated emphatically. "What's my name?"

He glanced down at his clipboard because he didn't know it. Then just like people have done all my life, he mispronounced it when he found it.

"Wendle Sippie," he uttered, already guessing his pronunciation was wrong.

I was looking over at the inductee bus. Willie looked at me with a resigned expression of submission as the bus began to pull out.

"I'm sure," I finally replied to his initial question.

Then turning, I quickly got on my bus to avoid more conversation with the corpsman. I realized that this day was not really about our health or well-being; it was a process to provide bodies for the military and proof of readiness for others like myself for the next draft round.

Chapter 4
JUMPING FROM THE FRYING PAN INTO THE FIRE

A lot happened over the next few years following my physical.

Like most young couples, Ginny and I committed to one another at the start of our intimate relationship. Our first sexual experience was in the back seat of my Volkswagen on senior prom night.

Birth control pills existed in the early '60s but were provided to teens only with parental permission. Asking permission was an admission that you were having sex, which wouldn't have gone over well with Ginny's parents. I have no doubt a physical confrontation would have occurred between her dad and me, and wedding plans would have been put in motion just in case. Nothing would be allowed to damage their Italian family's honor.

My mother constantly checked my underwear for cum stains and warned me to abstain. I could expect general meanness toward Ginny after that.

Mother couldn't afford to say much more beyond, "You play with fire; you're going to get burned,"

She ran off and got married early during her senior year of high school and managed to keep it a secret so she could graduate. During the late 1930s high school days, getting married before graduation made people conclude that there was a baby on the way. Even though, in her case, that was not so.

My father died just before I graduated from high school. I have no idea what he would have said. We never talked much, even during the many one-hour drives to Pittsburgh for his chemotherapy treatments. He was terminal with Hodgkin's disease and very ill from the radiation. We only had one memorable conversation that started when he expressed his disappointment that I was more like my mother; an Artist.

So, we were, having sex in my Volkswagen for the first time. Which was quite a physical feat, especially with her in a bulky prom dress and me in my tux studded dress shirt with bowtie, suspender trousers, and a cumber bun. With her knees up to her shoulders, I peeled away what seemed like endless layers of under-skirting until I reached the bare skin of her inner thighs. The rest is somewhat blurry, but I remember vividly seeing her dark pubic hair lit only by the dash lights. At that point, I was going in for the kill. Nothing was going to stop me. I managed to get only two strokes when I climaxed and mustered enough willpower to withdraw before ejaculating inside her. I cupped the head of my penis with my hand. It filled with cum which immediately leaked through my fingers and all over her belly. What a euphoric feeling! I had masturbated many times since I was eleven, but it never felt like prom night! I wanted so badly to insert my still, very erect penis into her vagina and go again. I did not do so for fear of pregnancy.

WE BELONG TOGETHER – ROBERT & JOHNNY

You're mine and we belong together
Yes, we belong together for all eternity
You're mine, your lips belong to me
Yes, they belong to only me for all eternity
You're mine, my baby and you will always be
I swear by everything I own you'll always, always be mine
(Mine, mine, be mine)
You're mine and we belong together
Yes, we belong together for all eternity

…

Anyway, my prom night climax was my instant addiction to sex. I was determined to do whatever it took to get a steady supply of condoms, which, in the 60s, we called "rubbers." If I had only managed to get a hold of condoms for the prom, I would have happily cum and perhaps gone a few more times with the lessened fear of pregnancy.

In those days, condoms were hard to come by for young men, and druggists kept them out of sight and behind the counter. If you were bold enough to ask for them, the druggist would begin asking embarrassing questions to discourage you. "What do you want them for?" "How are you going to use them?"

If you could withstand the questions without answering them, the druggist would then ask for a driver's license. Finally, telling you that he would sell them to you when you were older. The druggist was suggesting the age of 21, which he randomly imposed.

Sometimes you could find a seedy gas station outside of town with a wall dispenser of condoms, but you had to buy some gas to get the key to the men's room. And even then, the dispenser was often empty, and you were cheated out of your quarter. Of course, you couldn't ask for your quarter back because the station attendant would start asking the same questions as the druggist. In the end, the attendant claimed he had nothing to do with the dispenser and only made money by leasing the privilege to put it there.

That prom night ended my virginity, but I never asked Ginny if it ended hers, and I didn't care. I was now a man of the world with aroused masculine instincts, a fundamental purpose that felt really good, and a new mission to improve the quantity and quality of my intercourse.

I didn't know anything about sex, except for what information and sometimes misinformation I gathered from talking with other boys. Videotapes hadn't been invented yet, and there were no porno stores with these tapes for rent. Sex education was still taboo in schools. So, all I could rely on was my basic instincts which amounted to what felt good. Of course, feedback from Ginny would have helped. But, other than a few squeals when I did something wrong, like trying to do it doggie style, all I had was to guess what pleased her by listening to her breathing.

We were too young to get married, but that didn't stop us from feeling and acting like we were. I got accepted to Point Park College in Pittsburgh, 50 miles away, and I came home every weekend, rain or shine, to be with Ginny.

Love and sex were the same things to me. I don't know how I passed most of my courses. My thoughts were about her all the time. When I thought about her, I fantasized about other ways to have sex. And since sex was love to me, being without her all week meant being without love. I must have spent most of my time in class daydreaming with a boner.

Within two years, I earned a degree in Engineering Design. Upon graduation, I felt I had not learned much, but I at least knew how to look for and find answers to solve problems. I applied to at least six graduate schools and sent my resume to a few defense companies.

One other thing I learned was how to turn a solution to a problem into profit. I am referring to a steady supply of condoms. I partnered with an older classmate who would buy condoms by the gross. That was more than I could use, so I started selling them to other underage classmates for a dollar a piece. They would balk at the price, but when the choice was to ride bareback and take a chance or pay my fee, they paid. The partnership was lucrative and provided extra spending money for weekends with Ginny.

There weren't many job opportunities then, but the defense industry in other states was booming. Every week there were advertisements in the paper from defense contractors. They offered good pay and extraordinary benefits. One such contractor was General Dynamics Electric Boat in Connecticut. All I got from the advertisement was that they built ships. That was very exciting to me. They advertised in the Pittsburgh paper because the area was rich in engineering students but poor in job offerings. I figured they wouldn't find job candidates with shipbuilding experience in Pittsburgh, so I sent in my resume, promptly receiving a standard rejection. For only the cost of postage, I used a strategy to ignore the rejection and immediately sent another resume. Of course, I received another standard rejection. But, I had nothing to lose by repeating this process until someone in their personnel department took notice.

After about six tries, I finally received a request for an interview with all expenses paid, including airfare. They even made hotel reservations and arranged for transportation. The fact that Ginny and I weren't married meant she had to stay behind and wait to hear of the outcome.

Chapter 5

LEARNING TO KEEP MY NOSE CLEAN
AND MY MOUTH SHUT

The submarine plant was larger than most towns across Pennsylvania. Just the parking structures for the 18,000 employees seemed to go on forever. The transportation driver pulled over to the curb in front of a multi-storied brick office building surrounded by heavy metal fencing.

"This is your gate," the cabbie said.

I had already noticed that there were quite a few entrance gates manned with uniformed security guards.

"Try and remember it and how to get back to it, as this is where you are expected."

I thanked him, grabbed my briefcase of drawings for the interview, and walked to the nearest guarded gate, where two security guards stood.

"Your name?" said the guard with a clipboard.

"Weldon Sipe," I responded. "I have an interview."

The guard interrupted me. "You old enough to have a driver's license?"

The other guard snickered. "Yes," I responded.

"Let me see it, please." He looked at it. "He is here to see Randall Quantro," he quickly said to the other guard, who preceded to hand me a metal tray.

"Remove everything from your pockets and any jewelry," the second guard said.

Then he raised my arms and frisked me. He nodded to the first guard that I had nothing on me.

"Put your briefcase up here," he said, motioning to a steel table beside him. I did as he asked as the other guard finished patting me down.

"Open it, please," said the guard. I did, and he quickly checked the contents and then closed the briefcase.

"You will be escorted to Mr. Quantro," said the guard. "When you are through with your interview, you must be escorted back to this gate."

"Here are your personal things." He motioned to the tray.

But when I reached for my briefcase, he stopped me. "That stays here. You will get it back when you leave."

"It's only examples of my work," I said. "You won't need them," was his reply.

Judging from their indifferent and detached attitude, they oddly reminded me of the military physical I had several years earlier.

"Thank you," I said, hurriedly putting my things back into my pockets. As expected, there was no response from them.

I followed the guard into the building and up three flights of stairs. Even though there were more stairs, there were no indications of what floor you were on. We went through the door, and I was immediately overwhelmed by what I saw.

As far as I could see, there seemed to be thousands of employees sitting in parallel rows of long drafting tables stretched to all sides of the building. There were only narrow isles where you could walk, and they went the entire building length. There were no cubicles except a couple in the center of the far side of the room.

"Stay right behind me," commanded the guard as we proceeded quickly toward the cubicles on the other side of the room.

It was evident that this was a very solemn place to work. There was little conversation.

Most employees were bent over their tables at their assigned spots and busily drawing with mechanical drafting machines. These machines combined vertical and horizontal rulers rotating as a protractor and a robotic arm for precise layouts. I learned drafting with a wooden T-square in college. A separate plastic angle or a combination of angles was used to achieve the desired angle. So, this machine technology was a step up for me but not a challenge. The principles of drafting weren't different.

When we got to Randall Quantro's office, there was a lot of commotion. We were met by a frail older woman who looked like someone's grandma. The guard whispered something to her, and she turned to me.

"Have a seat, Mr. Sipe, she said softly. "I'll tell Mr. Quantro you're here."

There were no seats to sit in, so awkwardly, I remained standing. Just then, two men hurriedly came out of the office, and by the look on the first man's face, he was not very happy. I assumed it was Quantro right behind him.

"Don't bullshit me on the number of hours for that job, Taylor," he said piercingly to the first man out of the office as they charged past me.

"You need more men; I'll get you more men. Just don't bullshit me."

He turned to go back into his office and bumped into me. "What the fuck do you want?" he barked right into my face.

Before I could speak, the old woman meekly said, "This is Weldon Sipe. He's here for his interview."

"Then what the fuck are you doing out here! Get in my office and have a seat."

At first, I thought I had somehow mistakenly been put into the military. At the least, this was how I imagined the military would be because of my memories of the military physical.

His office reminded me of my principal's office in high school. It was very plain, painted battleship gray, and had a metal door with 'Randall Quantro, Superintendent, Nuclear Design Division,' on the door's window. There were other windows, but all of them were covered with drawn metal blinds. Most of the light came from the fluorescent ceiling lights that gave the room a cold green cast. He had a desk that he used for a chair that faced a row of a half-dozen gray metal chairs. It was evident to me that the room's fashion was to make everyone feel uncomfortable and stressed.

"So, you want to work in shipbuilding?" he probed when he finally returned to his office.

He casually looked through an opened manila file folder as he carried it to his desk. He promptly laid it down and sat on the edge of his desk in front of me.

"Yes, sir."

"Why do you want to leave Pennsylvania," he asked.

"There aren't a lot of jobs in the Pittsburgh area, and…

He interrupted any further elaboration, "What about your family?"

"My mother is the only one left at home of my immediate family." "You have a brother who's teaching in Maryland," he said.

That confirmed my suspicions that the file on his desk was about me.

"Yes," I replied, figuring that it was best to keep my answers short so as not to contradict anything I had written on my many applications.

"What does your mother think of your wanting to move to Connecticut?"

"She is well established in Pennsylvania and has a sister left there," I said.

He turned back to my file and flipped through it. I could tell from the number of pages that it contained more than just my application.

After silently gleaning a little more information, he said, "The Sipe's were steel makers, I see, except for your brother and you. You know much about steel?"

"My dad used to say, scrap in, metal out, and that's all you need to know."

He smiled. "We work on a need-to-know basis here too."

He closed my file on his desk and grimly turned back to me, asking, "You think you can follow directions, do what is asked of you, keep your nose clean, and your mouth shut?"

"Yes, sir," I replied without any hesitation.

"Okay," he said. "Ms. Marie," he called for his secretary.

The old woman was instantly there as if she was by the door expecting his summoning.

"Call Security and have him returned to his hotel room."

She promptly left the room. Quantro stood up. "We will let you know something very soon."

It didn't feel like a successful interview, especially when he didn't offer to shake my hand.

I felt I needed to try to salvage my chance to be hired, "I brought samples of my work, but the security guards kept my briefcase at the gate."

"We've already been supplied with all the information we need.

We'll be in touch within a few days."

As he stated, I received an offer letter from General Dynamics, Electric Boat Division, called EB, within a few days. I was now a nuclear designer on submarines for what seemed a good hourly rate. The letter said that I would need to start immediately, and that temporary low-cost dormitory housing would be provided until I made more permanent arrangements.

Chapter 6
WHAT ABOUT GINNY

Ginny and I hadn,t discussed marriage yet. I assumed we would eventually, but we were too young to get a marriage license. In Pennsylvania, the law was 21 unless parents gave signed permission at a licensing bureau. So openly, we discussed it because the job offer meant we would be separated for weeks at a time.

I felt it was best for me to get comfortable with the job and scope out the surroundings for possible places to live, and I would come home as often as possible. It was a 5 1/2-hour drive, and Ginny reluctantly agreed that we had no other choice.

I knew Ginny wanted to escape her family, especially her father. He was the typical flamboyant 1920,s male who had to rule the roost and protect his family and business interests. She wanted to have a life of her own. Still, I also knew that she would miss having everything she wanted given to her by her father. I was not his choice for Ginny as I was not Italian nor a self-made man. In short, I was not like him, with a loud and boisterous nature, always taking charge of the conversation and trying to force his opinions on everybody else. Ginny was firm about choosing me and made it clear that I was what he would get.

Chapter 7
MOVING TO CONNECTICUT

I was excited about moving to Connecticut and being on the ocean. I tried to get Ginny excited about her new life with me and talked about everything I saw and did on my weekend trips home.

It did not take me long to find an apartment on the New London side of the river and move out of the dorm provided by Electric Boat. So I could avoid the heavy traffic through the city of New London, I chose an apartment close to the bridge and near the river, where I spent a lot of time watching the boats and submarines while writing letters to Ginny. I had no furniture for the first few weeks, so I slept on the hardwood floor in a sleeping bag I brought from home.

On one trip home, I saw an ad for a sailboat in my hometown newspaper. It was a used sealed-hull square rigger sailboat, and you sit on it, not in it. It had a single sail hoisted up the mast on a spar or boom perpendicular or "square" to the mast.

This lightweight sailboat sat on 2 car rooftop racks and was only 10 feet long and 4 feet wide. The seller insisted it would fit on my Volkswagen. To my amazement, nylon rope tied the boat's bow and stern cleats snuggly to the front and back bumpers. While driving the speed limit on the turnpike, it felt like a wing was on top of the VW, and I would leave the ground. I stopped at several rest stops and checked the ropes to make sure the boat hadn't shifted. Everything was fine, and the boat's bow served as one gigantic visor blocking the sun and rain for the whole windshield.

CHAPTER 8

Getting My Feet Wet

I couldn't wait to try the boat out in open water rather than the small pond where I first tried to sail. As soon as I moved into the apartment, I took it down to the water. I had never seen a sailboat upstream from the interstate bridge the few times I had been there. Knowing very little about sailing, and in my naivety, I tried to sail alone to the bridge.

SLOOP JOHN B - The Beach Boys

We come on the sloop John B
My grandfather and me
Around Nassau town we did roam
Drinking all night
Got into a fight
Well, I feel so broke up
I want to go home
So hoist up the John B's sail
See how the main sail sets
Call for the captain ashore
Let me go home
Let me go home
I wanna go home, yeah, yeah
Well, I feel so broke up
I wanna go home
The first mate, he got drunk
And broke in the captain's trunk
The constable had to come and take him away

Sheriff John Stone

Why don't you leave me alone? Yeah, yeah

Well, I feel so broke up

I wanna go home

So hoist up the John B's sail (hoist up the John B's sail)
See how the main sail sets (see how the main sail sets)

Call for the captain ashore, let me go home
Let me go home
I wanna go home, let me go home

...

I drove down to the river's edge until the front wheels were submerged up to the hubcaps. Then, I unbuckled the boat from the car's roof rack and slid the boat down the hood and into the water. I raised the sail, put on my life jacket, and pushed off from shore. The tide was going out, and winds were sporadic; therefore, the current of the river's water was heading toward the bridge. The closer I sailed toward the concrete and steel structure, the more massive it looked.

The thought of hitting one of those piers horrified me.

Turning one side of the boat into the wind, then turning the other side into the wind, known as tacking, is a way of speedily moving the boat forward into an oncoming wind. Headway is achieved by zigzagging over what would be a straight line to where you want to go.

I was doing well on this attempt at sailing until the wind stopped, and then I started drifting backward. This was not good. Still drifting toward the bridge, I realized I would not have a choice but to go under it. I fearfully tried to keep the boat heading toward the open space between the cement piers. Still, without any wind, I could only use the boat's tiller to guide me where I wanted to go. As I got closer to the bridge, I could hear the cars and trucks overhead. The rumbling vibrated the air around me. The space between the piers seemed to get smaller and smaller, and the piers became more prominent and more disturbing. The boat started drifting toward one of them, which panicked me, so I laid down on the deck. Holding onto the deck grips, I extended my feet as far as possible to protect the boat from hitting the pier. The white sail was soon in the shadow of the bridge above, and the clear blue sky was blocked from my view. Certainly, I was going to glide into the cement pier. I prepared to push away from the pier using my legs while holding on tightly to the deck grips with my hands. My tennis shoes scraped the pier, and I successfully pushed the boat away from it as I drifted by. Suddenly in the sun, I felt a sense of relief. For the next few minutes, I lay on the deck looking at the sky, eventually gaining enough self-control to turn my attention to the shoreline to find a place to land. What was the point? There was still no wind, the sail was limp, and the current kept me in the center of the river.

I slowly drifted past an old broken-down barge left to rot along the neglected shore. A sudden gust of wind stretched the sail, and I grabbed the tiller preparing to turn around and head back toward the bridge. The wind suddenly stopped again, and the sail went limp as it fluttered and gasped for air.

The freshwater of the Thames River meets and mixes with saltwater from the Atlantic Ocean as the tide comes in and goes out. The Long Island Sound is the narrow portion of the Atlantic Ocean between the Connecticut coastline and Long Island. A sound is a body of water typically connected to a sea or ocean. The river's current won out and pushed the boat down the middle toward the open sound.

"No sense in panicking," I told myself aloud. "There is nothing I can do. I am not in control."

I laid down in the boat in total resignation and tried to appreciate the silence of the river and the clouds in the sky.

There was a faint whooshing sound off in the distance, but as it became louder, I turned my head in its direction to see what it was. Submerged in the water except for the observation tower, a nuclear submarine bore down on me! I panicked from the fear no one on board knew I was in its path. I tugged on the sailboat pulley and turned the rudder back and forth like an oar in frantic desperation, but it was too late. A wave of water passed over what little was visible of the submarine's mighty black steel hull. It lifted my sailboat and me out of the water, turned the boat over, and flipped me overboard. I swam back to my boat and held on for my life, my arms over the edge of the tipped sailboat as the dark black shadow of the submarine passed beneath me like a giant whale. The captain showed no signs of acknowledgment of my presence. The submarine was close enough, and I knew he was looking at me through the ship's periscope. The sub continued indifferently upriver as if I was not there, leaving me clinging to my swamped boat.

I waved my fist in the air and shouted, "I have the right-of-way, you bastards."

I felt eerie about what might be lurking beneath my feet in the dark brackish water. I tried uprighting the sailboat by standing on the centerboard on the underside and pulling the handrail on the deck toward me. The water-laden sail was impossible to lift. So, I swam to the other side and slid the sail down the mast. That brought the weight of the sail closer to the deck. As the water drained from the sail cloth, I could finally pull it up into the air and upright.

Only a few minutes passed when I heard another approaching boat. It was a Coast Guard patrol boat.

"You need a little help?" called out one of the sailors.

I hated to admit defeat, but I gratefully accepted their help.

"Yes, thank you. There's not enough wind to sail today," I said, thinking that was the reason no other sailboats were in the river.

"You might want to rethink where you choose to sail. Many sharks follow the fishing boats because of the chum, and enough salt water mixes with the freshwater of the Thames River." the Coat Guard Captain informed me.

I realized that I could have been shark bait. He threw me a tow rope.

"Point to where you want to beach," he shouted.

"Just on the other side of the bridge," I said, and away we went.

After several minutes we went under the bridge, and I pointed to my car. He slowed the patrol boat, made a sharp u-turned, and I drifted to the shore.

As I untied the tow line, he asked, "Do you sail much?"

"This is my first time," I lied to him.

"Well, here's some information for you." He tossed an envelope of information on the shore. "You might get some good pointers from it. Carefully read the rights-of-way rules for vessels."

"Thanks," I said, embarrassed. I knew right then that the submarine Captain must have notified them of my situation, and maybe he felt a little guilty.

I was exhausted and waterlogged, and I climbed on the deck and lay there to catch my breath.

The information that the Coast Guard gave me explained rights- of-way for vessels on the water. It is a general courtesy, not an actual law, that should be followed. What applied to me was that, generally, a sailboat should always keep out of the way of other large vessels in narrow channels because larger vessels may not have the room to be able to maneuver or change direction. That may be true, but I was not under power because there was no wind, and I am sure the submarine's captain observed that my sail was listless. He did have the ability to stop, or at least slow down, but he chose not to. I believe they were just having a laugh at my expense.

Chapter 9
THE NATURE OF A DEFENSE PLANT JOB

Entering the design and engineering building every day was always overwhelming. I managed to learn my way around the Nuclear Design Department the first couple of weeks, finally finding the toilet, the candy machine, and my section of a fifty-foot drafting table. There were no numbers or signs, so it was easy to become disoriented. There were 3000 designers on the third floor alone.

The men's room was referred to in the Navy lingo as the head or, most often, the shitter. The head was always easy to find because of the smell, and there was always a line.

Since smoking wasn't prohibited, the vending machines sold cigars in addition to candy. Cigarettes weren't popular. Cigars were preferred because it was a Connecticut thing. The state is one of the largest suppliers of cigar wrappers. The wrapper is the outermost leaf of the cigar, which has to be of perfect quality to hide the paper binder layer underneath that holds the cheap filling tobacco.

Over the next several months, I slowly got to know all the guys around me and their peculiarities. Levels of education and experience varied, but most designers around me had been job shoppers, meaning they had primarily worked on short-term or temporary contracts. Those jobs paid exceptionally well and often required them to work far from home while living in the EB area. The work they did could involve long hours and sometimes included seven-day workweeks. The result was they had houses paid off at a very young age.

Those that had established families and homes nearby, and had design experience related explicitly to piping systems, were sought out by EB. They settled for the company's lower pay scale, which they considered just comfortable enough to exchange their traveling lifestyle for the opportunity to stay home. A few came from military backgrounds. Some worked their way up from the yard or the area where the subs were actually being built.

The designers were all older than I, and most had no college degree. I was an exception to those generally employed, and they wondered why someone so young was hired. After all, I couldn't even buy a beer. This explains why I got the nickname "College Wonder Boy," I suppose.

At first, the jobs I was given seemed trivial. They came as "change orders" and included basic instructions on what to alter on the drawings without any elaboration or additional explanations. Usually, making changes or additions to the general notes or random changes to numbers and references was all that was involved in the jobs assigned to me.

My supervisor was an overweight, hurried, bluster-voiced man who was always short on explanations. He seemed on the verge of anger, but he was nice enough to me because I think he was probably intimidated by my education. He was never without a cigar in his mouth, and he chewed on the butt all day long, rarely lighting one. You could tell he was agitated when he started biting hard.

One morning, he came over to me with a large bundle of plans in his arms. The plans came in three-foot widths and unrolled to up lengths of fifty feet.

"Start erasing all references to the 593, pronto," he said as he plopped them down in front of me and walked off. "There's a lot more plans to come."

I took one of the plans from the stack and located the reference block. It was the obvious place to start because it referred to the coordinates of the SSN593 THRESHER areas on the drawing. Using my electric eraser, I removed all the references to SSN593.

I had hardly finished the first drawing from the stack when the supervisor brought another large bundle of drawings and added it to the stack.

"When you're done with those, here are some more," he said.

"Why are we erasing all records of the Thresher?" I asked.

"We do it for defense, for the defense of our country!" He started biting on his cigar, and I knew I should not have questioned him and kept quiet. "Eternal vigilance is the price of freedom. You're old enough now, college boy, to know what it means to fight for what you've got. No one is going to fight for you, sure as hell. You married?"

I knew he expected me to say something, so I said the only answer that came to mind. "Well, not yet."

"You're not going to let any son-of-a-bitch take your wife, are you? See what I mean? The war effort. In this business, boy, we're always at war, just like in marriage, and it's always a fight. Always. And don't you forget it."

I kept working as I had no idea what he was talking about. He left, and I said loud enough to be heard by

George and Tom on the drafting table in front of mine, "For the love of God, I don't understand that man."

Tom laughed.

George turned around. "What was old fish face saying? The usual crap about eternal vigilance?"

"Yeah, I guess," I replied, astonished. "So why am I erasing all references to the Thresher?"

"Because it sank, dumb ass," George responded sarcastically and to the point as always. George was a little guy with a larger-than-life voice and squinting eyes that were crossed just enough that I always wondered how he could make changes to drawings.

Tom laughed at his remark. "We didn't build it. It's a Portsmouth boat." Tom always agreed with George, and he was the kind of guy who always talked with his teeth clenched. When he raised his voice, it was easy to think he was angry.

I thought for a moment and realized that making these changes the way I did wouldn't leave a traceable record. The correct procedure would have been to draw a line through the words rather than erasing them. This job didn't even come with a change order; consequently, there was no record of the change request.

"Yeah, but ifit's referenced, something must be similar to ..." I started to make a case about not following procedures.

"Look, college boy," George interrupted me, "we didn't build that ship, so just get it the fuck off there, okay!"

Tom turned toward George laughing a little, but he noticed the supervisor was coming back. "Stow it. Fishface is coming." Nonchalantly, they all turn to their work. The supervisor approached me again.

"How many of those plans reference valves would you say?"

"Most, I think," I said as I started to unroll another plan.

"Better get familiar with all of them, pronto. A Navy Officer is coming to ask you some questions."

"Why me?"

"Because you have the plans. Just answer his questions, and don't look to me for help," my supervisor stated emphatically.

"Suppose I can't answer a question? What do I say?" I countered.

"They're probably just sending the poor bastard on a routine fishing expedition," snapped the supervisor biting hard on his cigar butt and quickly leaving.

George turned around. "He thinks he's Uncle Sam's right arm. Right arm, my ass! He's only the super here cause his wife is the department head's sister. That's his extent of the war effort. Uncle Sam, my ass."

"Don't you like this job?" I asked. "They pay you well. And it's, well, patriotic work, defense work."

They both laughed at my comment. "Patriotic! Shit!" exclaimed George. "What the hell difference does that make?"

"Yeah, what the hell?" repeated Tom.

"And there's no such thing as defense work in the defense business. This is war business, and we make monster subs that deliver nuclear missiles hopefully before the boat sinks," George stated.

They both turned back to their work. George mutters, "If they're lucky, they make it home."

I learned my lesson never to think we were in the defense business. I promptly changed the subject. "Is he serious about the Navy Officer? I don't know very much about these plans. There must be a hundred valves on them. What do I do...?"

"You ain't never been in the service, have ya?" said Tom through his clenched teeth.

"No, Tom, he's one of those college wonder boys, remember?" said George. "It's no wonder he don't know nothin'. That's why he's a wonder boy."

"Look, wonder boy," said Tom, "the Navy officer probably doesn't know the difference between a design plan and an interoffice memo."

"Why do you think it costs 60 million to build a submarine?" asked George. "It costs 10 million to build the actual boat, another 5 million to adhere to the Company's bullshit specs that force us to use only their incestuous group of suppliers. And another 30 million for the blowjob it takes to explain it all to the Navy."

"Go see Harry," Tom said to me. "Harry will know if there is more to it than Fishface is telling."

"Trust us," added George.

"Who's Harry?" I asked.

Tom informed me, "Harry knows everything about everything and everybody. He keeps our noses clean. In case you didn't notice, all your change orders are probably signed by him."

"Where do I find Harry?"

Chapter 10
MORE THAN MEETS THE EYE

It didn't take me long to find Harry. He was on the same floor but quite a distance away. He was an older gentleman, and a big man with a voice of authority, even though he spoke softly.

As I approached him, he spoke without looking up. "Yes?"

"My name is Weldon Sipe. I work in the piping section."

"I know who you are. What can I do for you?"

I couldn't help but notice he was redlining blueprints the whole time we spoke and only made eye contact when he had something important to say. I relayed the pending visit from a Navy officer, and he listened intently.

"It's routine," he said. "Nothing to worry about."

"But what do I do if I can't answer his questions?" He turned to me and made eye contact.

"You went to college? Do just what you did on a college exam when you don't know the answer. Guess. He won't know what you're talking about. They can't build subs, but they officially authorize our work, so they have to make it appear they are overseeing what we do by making routine visits and asking stupid questions." After a pause, "Anything else?"

"No, I guess not," I replied.

"I haven't seen your name on the union roster yet. Why is that?"

"It doesn't make sense to me to join," I replied. "We can't strike."

"Oh, we can. We just never have to." Again, making eye contact, this time more intense, "You've heard the expression when mama is happy, everyone is happy?"

"Yes."

"Well, if the union is happy, everyone is happy. Cause if it's not, the government, the Navy, and EB won't be happy."

I believed that the union would give the membership a unified voice. And that a unified labor rally could favor EB or the Navy when it came to contract negotiations with the government for a new submarine.

For the company and the Bureau of Ships, having a union contract assured them that the design force and the labor power were prepared to fulfill the proposed design and build requirements.

Still, after working there just a few months, I realized that the union members only really cared about their wages and benefits. They had nothing to lose by playing one big power against the other, depending on which side offered the better deal. In reality, they were the biggest bully. So, I joined the union, but I felt my hands were dirty.

Chapter 11
THANKS...

I missed Ginny, and finally, I was so horny I became motivated to do something about it. The job was going well as far as I could tell, and I knew I was part of something big, much bigger than me.

My next trip home was Thanksgiving weekend. I convinced Ginny that since her dad wouldn't ever approve of us getting married at such a young age, we should make a fast trip to West Virginia and get married. She wasn't enthusiastic because she wanted a big wedding. But she wanted to go to Connecticut badly enough that she went along with it. The age requirement in West Virginia was 18, and there was no waiting period, physical exam, or blood test requirements.

We filled out the paperwork at the County Clerk's Office at the courthouse in Wheeling and got our license. There was a Chaplin within the courthouse complex, and he married us right there. We got back around 3 a.m., but her parents and my mother were so used to us being together and out late they never noticed.

Chapter 12
...BUT NO THANKS

I never ate much when visiting Ginny's family, especially the Thanksgiving we got married. Her father's Italian demeanor and references to his wealth intimidated me. Sitting at such an elaborate dining table, in a very ornate dining room and being served by kitchen help, all added to my discomfort. I was expected to act a certain way or do certain things without knowing what they might be.

I hoped this meal would go more smoothly than usual because I was going to tell them that we were married and she was moving to Connecticut with me. I pondered how to begin telling them the news when Dorothy began talking about Willie.

Willie was home. He had completed basic training and was now in the National Guard. We thought Willie would continue to work for his dad and go to weekend camp once a month with the boys, but the military had other plans for the National Guard. He had just received orders that he was being transferred to Indiana.

"It's going to be lonely around here without William," said Dorothy.

Dorothy barely understood the first time you explained something. Initially, I thought her elevator didn't go all the way to the top. I realized that because Earl was so overbearing, Dorothy never had the chance to think for herself.

"I thought you said going into the National Guard would protect William from..."

"I know what I said," snapped Earl. "You don't have to remind me!"

She gave him a confused look, and he took a deep breath to explain it to her one more time.

"The original plan was for him to serve his country while continuing to learn the business and work for me."

"Actually, it was to avoid the war," interjected Willie. "They aren't calling up the reserves for Viet…."

"Let's not look at it that way, William," Earl interrupted. "Technically, only in the event of a war do they have the right to call you up anytime."

"Dad's plan didn't work, in other words," said Willie as a matter of fact.

"That's what we get for voting in a Republican," barked Earl.

"I see," I said sarcastically. "So, they've called you up for active duty?"

"Yeah. I'm pretty certain I'm going to Vietnam."

Dorothy began sobbing and wiped the tears from her eyes with her napkin.

Earl's Italian demeanor kicked in, and he took the Vietnam call to duty as disrespect to his family because he hadn't chosen that path for his son. "I sure won't be giving large sums of money to those bastard's campaign next time," he growled.

There was a moment of awkward silence. It was apparent to me that none of this was Willie's choice.

"Well, as long as we're on the subject of choices...." I started to speak.

"Do you think this is a good time, Weldon?" interjected Ginny. "I mean..."

"It's as good a time as any," I replied emphatically.

"You're going to get married!" said Dorothy with sudden jubilation.

"We already did," I said to the point. "Last night." "What!" said Dorothy in astonishment.

"How could you do that?" Earl chimed in. "I didn't sign for a license."

"We drove to Wheeling yesterday," I retorted, staying on point.

I watched Earl begin to inflate like a blow fish. But instead of exploding, he only exhaled and said, "We'll go see Father Lutz tomorrow and get you properly married."

"We were properly married." I remarked. "Not in the eyes of the church," refuted Earl.

"Who's church? I'm not Catholic. And neither is God!"

Here we go, I thought, more spouting of the beliefs of the Catholic Church and that they are the ultimate authority, and they alone speak for God. But Ginny came to the rescue.

"That doesn't really matter, does it, daddy? Besides, you never go to church." That left him speechless. "I'm leaving for Connecticut with him."

I never imagined Earl to be wordless, but considering Willie was most likely going to Vietnam, I had some empathy for him. It turned out to be true that Willie was being shipped to Vietnam.

As the demand for more troops exponentially grew, Willie found himself transferred to yet another unit and then immediately deployed to Saigon just before Christmas. From there, it was into the jungle in teams of six, and that was the last we got news of him.

Chapter 13
ADJUSTING TO MARRIED LIFE

Our wedding night on the road to Connecticut served as our honeymoon and was not a momentous occasion. I had planned to go to a resort in the Poconos. She just wanted to keep going to get away from Pennsylvania as fast as possible. This was her first time away from home, except for one trip to Indiana to visit relatives when she was about three.

Going the entire distance meant that we wouldn't arrive until almost sun-up. Ginny started nodding off around midnight, and I was fading fast. The only motel we could find with a vacancy at such a late hour was a mobile home motel that looked like a trailer park.

I had trouble staying awake while waiting for her to come out of the bathroom. I concentrated on the good sex I was expecting and fantasized about ways to excite her and make her happy for marrying me. Ginny was my only sexual encounter, and I hoped she would take the lead and show me what she wanted. My hope was soon dashed. As it turned out, neither of us was very knowledgeable about having sex. This was our first time without a condom. Her vagina felt heavenly to me. Feeling her warm, lubricated skin soon brought me to a climax. I exploded inside her, releasing all my cum.

"Well, that was better than sex in the VW," I said, reassuringly. I was completely in the dark about how to understand her sexual needs.

"It's all right," she responded. "I'm just tired."

I lay there for a while, letting my heart rate slow. Ginny turned her back to me, but I knew she was restless by her constant tossing and turning and irregular breathing. I got a glimpse of her backside as she pulled the covers up. She had a sexually alluring shape and pure white skin. Aroused again, I wanted to pull her body into me and have her again. I snuggled up to her but got no response. I had finished but was by no means satisfied. Eventually, I gave up and fell asleep.

The following day, I proposed that we go sightseeing, but she wanted to head straight to the apartment. I gave up on having a honeymoon.

To my surprise, she liked the apartment, even as sparsely furnished as it was. Until her bedroom furniture arrived from Pennsylvania, we had to sleep on a new mattress on the floor that I had purchased.

Married life was a monumental change for both of us. I guess we didn't know each other as well as we thought, or at least as well as I thought. Our life together up until then was dating and sex. Lots of sex. She seemed less interested in sex with each passing day. Maybe I was looking at it all wrong. We were just getting used to being around each other and taking care of all the petty details that married life brings. Life was so much simpler when we had sex on the run, so to speak, and only on the weekends. So, I rationalized that sex wasn't as thrilling when it's always in front of you for the taking.

Chapter 14
THE STAKES GET HIGHER

When I returned to work as a married man, I realized immediately that everyone else knew I got married, and their attitude toward me had changed. Most notably, the supervisor began to give me more challenging assignments.

The first day back was one of my most exciting at Electric Boat.

The day the direction of my life would change.

First up was an order to design a valve that would meet all applicable Navy specs found within twelve thick volumes of information. It took me a week to glean the needed information and to begin a design. The big question was how much space was available in the vicinity where the valve was to go.

A blueprint schematic was attached to the work order, but the piping systems on it looked like a bowl of spaghetti. I decided to make a trip to the mock-up and see where the valve was to be placed.

In the days before computers with 3D design software, the mock-up was a life-size model of the submarine's interior made up of hundreds of pieces of wood representing valves and runs of pipelines. Even the bulkheads, hatches, and instrumentation were represented by similarly shaped wood. The idea was to avoid interference between objects and make the best use of allotted space for piping and support systems. This mock-up was for the USN-671, a unique design that would include many innovations, unlike any previous submarine design.

Heading from the design building toward the yard, I could hear some strange chanting. A bizarre-looking group of people had gathered outside the iron security gate. They were all dressed in plain white robes, and their heads were shaved except for a ponytail. Their chanting and dance-like movements led me to believe they were celebrating or protesting the day's scheduled launch of the last Polaris ballistic missile submarine, USS Will Rogers. There was no way to get close to the protestors, so I continued on to the mockup, intending to find out about the protestors when I returned to the design building.

I had to squeeze through several bulkheads to get to the correct compartment, following the little information provided on the incomplete piping system schematic. The numerous wooden parts of the mockup were hand-labeled according to how they were probably referred to on the various original design drawings, which I didn't have access to. It was impossible to make sense ofwhat I was looking at. So, I was resigned to looking for any referenced pipeline indicated on the schematic. When I found a pipeline reference number, I followed it to find a space available for the valve.

It took a long time to make my way through the cramped spaces and maneuver around all the other piping systems, but the reference number for the pipeline kept me on track. I also noticed numbers on other piping pieces like valves, elbows, and connectors. As I crawled along, I verified them to what few were indicated on the schematic.
Finally, I matched a piping part, indicating I was very near the end of the line and the probable spot for my valve.

When I got to the right place, there was no available space because a mock-up block of wood representing what I was to design was already there! This meant a valve had already been installed on the actual system.

"What the hell!" I said out loud. "Son-of-a-bitch!"

All the work I had done so far was in vain. I was disgusted enough to take a walk before returning to the design department.

The actual submarine hull under construction was surrounded by catwalks. Catwalks are an elaborate makeshift system of switchback metal walkways to the top.

Two men were up ahead of me in a heated discussion. As I got closer, I heard some of what they were saying.

"This has nothing to do with the Union, Bill. No one's sure what brought that sub down."

The other worker noticed that I was approaching them and motioned to the one speaking to hold up the conversation. It was uncomfortable squeezing past them, knowing they were intentionally waiting until I was out of earshot. The vocal worker was overanxious to make his point and did not wait.

"Someone's got to blow the whistle on this launching before the same failure happens on other subs."

The other worker was still staring at me and trying to delay the conversation until I was out of range. He lowered his voice level, but I could still hear him because the sound echoed off the submarine's hull.

"It probably isn't something serious," he said matter of factly. "They'll find out what it is during the shakedown.

And besides, we'll get a bonus for delivery ahead of schedule."

"Choke on your fucking bonus," snapped the other worker.

"Vote right, eat right, eh?" the other worker tried to make light of the conversation. "Lighten up, will ya? You sound like a commie, you know that? Your concern for the common man is touching, but our job is only to make sure ..."

I was having trouble hearing any more of their conversation, but I think I heard the worker finish with, "...those missiles get off before the sub goes down."

As much as I was allowed, I walked up and around the hull of another sub that was being welded together. I then headed for the office building. I passed the USS Sturgeon that had been docked since its launch the previous February. It would take at least a year to load and connect all of its equipment before the submarine would be turned over to the Navy. As I was passing, a commotion started on the gangplank. A military sentry was blocking someone from boarding the vessel.

"I'm sorry, but you don't have the proper identification," said the sentry stoically.

"Do you know who I am, sailor?" hollered the little white-haired gentleman loudly while nose-to-nose in the guard's face.

"Yes, Sir. I think you are Admiral Rickover, Sir."

"You think, or you're sure?"

"I'm sure, sir."

"Then step aside," the Admiral said insistently.

By this time, a small crowd of yard workers had grouped together a safe distance from the Admiral's wrath.

"The rules state ..." said the sentry.

"The rules!" interrupted Rickover yelling at the guard but playing to the crowd. "The rules are a substitute for rational thought. You seem like a rational man, so I'll ask you one more time to step aside."

"I'm sorry, Sir," the sailor said, trying to keep from peeing his pants. "I can't let you board without proper identification."

Rickover paused for a moment, deciding the sentry's fate.

"You have made your choice to be among the other lowest common denominators of human society. Well, God may forgive you, son, but the bureaucracy of the Navy won't."

And with that, the Admiral stormed off.

I had finally calmed down from the drama I had witnessed by the time I got back to the design department. Rumors were already flying around that Rickover had sent the sentry on sea duty for two years. That may have actually been true, as no one ever saw that sailor again.

"Something's screwed up with this assignment," I said, frustrated. "I've spent a whole week designing a valve, and there's already one installed there!"

"That's why they made electric erasers," Tom said mockingly. "You'll use them a lot. Trust us."

From out of nowhere, Taylor appeared. After only a few words, it was evident that he was drunk. Taylor staggered down the aisle. I had seen him like this once before. It was a mystery where he was hiding his booze. He would leave for short periods at a time, just enough to have a quick nip, and then return. He heard Tom say, "trust us," and staggered over to me.

"You don't trust us, college boy? He burped. "Why ... why we're just one big happy family."

"The wind blew, and the shit flew, and in walked Mr. Happy," said George mockingly.

Taylor was too drunk to comprehend and just stood over me mindlessly.

"Hitting the happy sauce again, Taylor?" queried George.

"What do you mean hitting? He fell in," added Tom.

Taylor was outraged that we all knew he was drunk and headed for his stool to avoid further harassment.

"Aaaaahhhh," and then he burped, "Get off my back about that stuff. I don't drink and...," he lost his thought for a moment, "...and you know it."

"You're going to get canned, you know that," said George emphatically. "How are you goin' to feed those six ugly kids of yours then? Uh?"

"They won't fire me. I know too much," replied Taylor. "I seen too much. I been here too many years..."

George noticed that the super was coming and made a throat- clearing noise to alert the rest of us, which Taylor didn't pick up on.

As we all turned back to our work, George said to Taylor in a low tone, "Stow it."

Taylor still didn't pick up on the clue, but he should have felt the shadow of the super standing next to him.

"...and never once stepped out of line," finished Taylor, burping again.

Unfortunately, the smell of another burp didn't help his credibility. "I do exactly as they tell me to," he muttered.

At least Taylor was smart enough to pretend not to notice the super standing beside him. He didn't look up at him, only down at the drawing board.

"I never step out of line," he grumbled.

But it was too late. The super leaned into Taylor and spoke into his ear.

"You're fired, Taylor. I warned you, didn't I? I warned you!"

Taylor did not respond.

"You listening to me? You're a risk. A risk to Electric Boat and the country for that matter."

Stated risk factors were causes for firing anyone. It meant you could never have grounds to come back.

Within moments, security personnel showed up to escort Taylor out of the design department.

The super stormed off, and we all turned to Taylor. Taylor gathered some of his tools from the top of his drafting table and carefully put them in his briefcase.

One of the security guards stopped him from packing up more things.

"Just leave everything here. Come with us." Finally, without looking up, he spoke to us.

"Tell the super I'll pick up the rest of my things tomorrow or the next day."

No one answered him. We were still in shock. None of us had witnessed a senior designer get fired from a government job, especially with a union behind him. Taylor wanted an answer.

"Will you do that for me? Will you tell the super?"

"Sure, Taylor. Sure. Your things will be at the gate. You know you won't be allowed to come back here."

"Probably not," responded Taylor. He removed his baseball cap from his cabinet and put it on his head. Then, as he began to leave, "Tell the super I'll see him in hell along with the rest of you boys. No offense."

George felt empathy for him. After all, he was guilty of taking a nip of vodka on the job. He showed me once that all you had to do was fill an orange with vodka using a syringe until it was ready to bust. Then, conceal the orange in your lunch box until break time.

"Take care of those six ugly kids now, hear," remarked George.

Taylor was marched past row after row of designers until he was out of site.

"One big happy family," muttered Tom. "Just one big happy family."

All was silent for the next few moments. We were all thinking about what had just happened and wondering if there was something we could do. For me, it was a moment of realization that I was nothing more than a cog within the gears of the military-industrial machinery.

A moment later, the silence was broken when a young, clean-cut Navy officer came down the aisle and called my name.

"Wendle Sippie?" he said while studying a piece of paper in his hand.

"Weldon Sipe?" I said, correcting him.

"Yes," he said.

He looked up from the piece of paper he used to prompt himself. "Are you working on the valve plans for the 640 Class?"

"Yes, Sir." I could feel my adrenalin kicking in as my face flushed when he approached and stood beside my stool. I became instantly nervous when he looked at his paper again and read a question.

"Could you show me what valves are going to be used on the 3000 PSI water supply system?" the Officer asked.

I could tell he was as nervous as I was, and it was the moment of truth to find out if Harry was right about his ignorance of the subject.

I hesitated a moment and repeated part of the question, "3000 PSI water supply."

"Yes," he responded confidently while glancing at his paper to ensure he had asked it correctly.

For an instant, and only an instant, I wondered if I could actually answer his question as it was asked. I realized that couldn't be because there were numerous 3000 PSI water supplies on a submarine. But which valve, on which system, and where the hell might it be found. Oh well, here goes, I thought.

We were just two rookies in the shipbuilding field, placed in a position of authority over something neither of us knew much about. I was sure I heard my two co-workers snicker in the background as I, with my false confidence, tried to help this officer.

I then reached over to a stack of plans beside me. Knowing that I had no idea what I was looking for, I fumbled through the stack like I was searching for a specific plan and pulled one out. I removed the rubber band and unrolled the plan quickly, so the Officer didn't notice the title block and other identifying information. I continued unrolling it for about fifteen feet until I saw several valves. I glanced over what was there for a few seconds, then put a finger on one of them.

"All will be similar to this Wallworth J-106 with optional hand wheels, of course," I said to baffle him.

The tenseness reached new heights for me as the Officer studied the valve in silence. I would have been caught in my lie if he had challenged me. Tom and George were anticipating my failure and listened for the silence to be broken. I thought that I had been set up for failure.

"Yes. Different hand wheels, of course," the Officer suddenly said.

At that moment, I realized he didn't know what he was looking at or if I had answered his question.

"Very good," he said as he looked up and took a few steps back. "Very good," he said again as he made some kind of notation on his paper.

Tom and George turned somewhat toward me to witness the situation's absurdity. The Officer apparently was satisfied. He took a few steps backward and saluted me.

There was some subdued chuckling from George and Tom, amazed at the Officer saluting a civilian. I didn't know what to do, so I haphazardly saluted back, prompting a few more chuckles. With paper in hand, the Officer left quickly.

"Just one big happy family," Tom said cynically under his breath, alluding to the fact that no one would step up to support anyone in any situation.

A moment later, the wall horns blasted loudly, informing all that it was lunchtime. Everybody was ready for the lunch break because we had prepared for it all morning. It was like a horse race when the horns sounded. Lunch pails, bags, and thermoses suddenly appeared out of nowhere. Chess boards and pieces were set up, and decks of cards being shuffled were heard in all directions. Cribbage was the favorite card game.

"Come on, wonder boy, I'll buy you a hotdog," said George. "You deserve a prize today for having balls."

Like stampeding cattle, the lunch crowd exited the building and headed toward the security gates. Outside the gates, the street was lined with the usual catering trucks, and employees hovered around them like bees to a hive to get lunch items. That day it was overly crowded. More employees than usual came out to see the group of protesters that had doubled in size since I had seen them earlier. They were down the street to where the shipyards' gates stood.

I told them about overhearing two employees in the yard discussing a submarine that just sank. And that maybe I should tell someone about it. Both George and Tom nixed that idea.

"It doesn't matter what you heard," said George. "It'll come out in the wash."

"So, what, dummy, if they stop building ships. Just vote right and eat right," said Tom satirically.

"Stow it, Tom. The college boy don't understand nothin! He's a set-up for eternal vigilance. He don't know the difference between eatin' right and patriotism. He's working for defense, remember?"

"Don't try and understand it," Tom said to me. "Just do as we say. We ain't never steered you wrong, have we?"

Like sheep, we were herded through the last security gate leading onto the street at lunchtime. Everyone had to be careful not to talk until they were out of range of the security guards. If the guards thought you were discussing business, you would be sent to the FBI office for questioning, and you weren't paid for your interrogation time.

The food trucks had a wide array of offerings, including grinders, a New England style submarine sandwich, candy, and other junk food. We got our hot dogs the most popular way, topped with sauerkraut and mustard, and then finished lunch with ice cream cones.

I stayed with George and Tom as we wandered down the street toward the crowd of protesters. The employees stared at them as if they were watching a circus freak show trying to understand why they were there. It felt like they were an affront to our livelihoods.

Many protesters were carrying peace signs and flaunted them in the workers' faces. Some joined in circles; others scattered among the gathering employees trying to pass out literature. The crowd got edgy as those from the design department realized that they were not only in total opposition to the submarine launching but desired to convert as many as possible to their pacificist way of thinking.

Suddenly behind us, there were sounds of police sirens approaching. State police came swarming out of prisoner wagons, dressed in riot gear with nightsticks, shields, and shielded helmets.

One black pacifist approached us, handed me a pamphlet, and then tried to hand Tom one. Tom snapped up the pamphlet, immediately took a bite out ofit, chewed a little, and spit it out. Then he crumbled up the rest of it and threw it into the protester's face.

"Goddam peacemonger. You can shove this up your ass, Uncle Sambo."

"There's your patriotism, sonny," barked George. "Goddam niggers and commies."

A husky black worker nearby overheard George. "Hey, who are you calling nigger, cracker?"

George cowered after glancing over at the massive yard laborer and seeing his size.

Still, he continued, barely audible, determined to make his point. "Hang 'em all by their balls. That's what the government ought to do. Hang 'em all by their balls."

About thirty police formed a line side-by-side that stretched across the street and divided the protesters from us.

"I think they want us to get the fuck out of the way," George declared.

"I think you're right," agreed Tom.

I folded my pamphlet and put it in my pocket. Then we joined the rest of the employees who began moving back towards the gates to open a path for the police. They were moving forward, taking small marching steps in cadence. The sound of their boots hitting the pavement rose above the employees' noise and the protesters' chanting.

"I think it's time to get back to work before we get beat over the head," said George emphatically.

"I think you're right again," said Tom smiling.

As we turned to head toward the office gate, I spotted Taylor walking into the parking structure. I wanted to say goodbye to him, so as the crowd gathered at the gate, I slipped away from George and Tom without notice.

I caught up with him on the top floor of the parking garage as he was putting his briefcase into the trunk of his car. "Taylor. Hey, Taylor," I hollered to him.

As I got closer, he seemed pretty sober but unwilling to talk. "Listen, Taylor, I don't think it was right."

"The Supervisor did me a favor," interrupted Taylor. "I couldn't take it anymore."

"What do you mean?"

"This place drove me to drink," he replied. "Hour by hour. Day by day."

The sound of the crowd in the street became noticeably louder, which caught Taylor's attention. He walked over and climbed up on the parking structures parapet wall that overlooked the yard and street below. I headed toward

Taylor, not quite sure if he might jump or if he would lose his footing from the aftereffects of his drinking.

"Maybe you can get some help someplace," I blurted out as I prepared to leap for his legs. "You can lick your problem."

"Get some help?! I don't need any help. Don't you see? Doesn't anybody see what's happening here?" Taylor balanced himself on the parapet wall and moved like a tightrope walker toward the front of the parking structure.

"Don't do anything stupid!"

Taylor ignored me and leaned over dangerously to see the street below. Not trusting his intentions, I slowly and cautiously climbed up on the edge with him and looked out over the submarine plant and onto the street below. My eyes were first drawn to the hubbub around the Will Rogers submarine, which was to be launched later that day.

The sub's bow was being draped with a ceremonial version of the American flag in preparation for the ceremony.

"They want to double, maybe triple, the number of missiles per sub in the future," said Taylor. "We have enough nuclear weapons now to destroy the whole damn world ten, maybe twenty times over. When is enough, enough?"

"Maybe they'll think twice before trying anything on us," I said.

"Your naive, Weldon. Do you think for one second that having the world's greatest military firepower will persuade any country that we should be feared? It's impossible to convey that we mean any sort of peace when they're staring down the barrels of our guns."

I didn't have a response to Taylor's profound words. After a long pause, he continued on.

"If we ever use nuclear missiles, we will only destroy ourselves! If any of us survive that kind of war, we will die slowly from eating poisoned food and drinking poisoned water. Those who die instantly will be the lucky ones."

Again, I had nothing to say.

"But then, we don't have the need to know, do we?" Taylor added, mimicking the need-to-know signs plastered on our walls at work.

"I'm sick of this need-to-know crap," I responded. "For a country that's supposed to be free, it's starting to feel less and less like it is."

"Well, when you start questioning things, it tells me there's still hope for you."

"What do you mean?"

"Look, college boy, you're just a firing squad member. You've been given a gun and told it's most likely loaded with blanks. But someone has been issued a gun that has a live round. No one knows who fired the fatal shot when the command is given to fire. Therefore, only one man has sinned by killing, and no one will ever know whom. We can all live at peace, remaining ignorant of knowing who killed the victim."

"So?" I retorted.

"Don't you see?" he replied. "We are all guilty. Each of us is a piece of the puzzle, part of the military-industrial complex. You're told to do a job and are not permitted to see or even talk about the whole picture. You cannot question, and you cannot pass judgment. You assume you are always firing a blank. They fill you with false pride and pay you well, too well. They buy your soul with a big house, a fancy car, health insurance, and a pension. These are the rewards for not asking questions and for not daring to think for yourself."

"It seemed like a good idea to work for national defense," I said, mulling over what he was saying. The pay is good."

"Ah, yes, the profit motive," uttered Taylor. "The sole basis of our economic system and the reason we go on believing the government propaganda that it's for our defense. Defense against who? What?"

"There's nothing wrong with making money, is there?"

"Is money your inspiration?" he barked again. "Do you judge your success by your salary?"

"Well, I ... "

"Don't be blind, Weldon. You're part of something evil here. Get out while you can before the evil that you have been exposed to changes you. Find something else to do. Be more concerned about making a life than making a living."

Just then, some rumbling sounds came from the street below. Taylor stepped closer to the edge of the wall, directly overlooking what was happening below.

"Can't you see we've all been indoctrinated into believing that security will be achieved through superior force?" he said in an almost empathetic sounding voice.

The rumbling got loud enough to get my attention. I carefully stepped onto the parapet wall to stand beside Taylor. Below, the office workers partly surrounded the pacifists. The yard workers had gathered against the gates waiting for the lunch whistle to blow.

"Violence rules the earth," Taylor said. "Our enemies won't seek peace out of fear of our weapons. They'll only hate us more. They'll defy our power with every opportunity they get in any inventive way they can think of. To them, we are the biggest deterrent to world peace."

The number of yard workers doubled within moments of the buzzer signaling the end of our lunch and the beginning of theirs. They were big, mean, and full of anger. The yard workers were already shouting at the pacifists before the yard gates were opened. The gates suddenly opened, and within seconds they lined the entire street like a pack of wolves encircling their prey. They were hanging on the gates, and some were also on the buildings' rooftops.

"Look at the lambs," said Taylor. "In their innocence, they are about to discover that making peace is as costly as war, as disruptive, and as liable to bring disgrace, prison, and maybe death."

The pacifists began singing, "We Shall Overcome."

"I don't know who they are, where they came from, or what they believe in, but I know that somehow they got it right," summarized Taylor in response to what we were seeing.

The number of stick-armed police formed a line at the crowd's edge. The police surrounded and pushed the pacifists into the yard workers.

"They'll stop the protest, won't they?" I asked, referring to the police. "I mean, the yardmen will kill them!"

Taylor didn't answer.

The police began beating their riot sticks against their shields in cadence while staying in a line formation in the distance. It looked like they were purposely showing force but made no attempt to interfere.

"They're just standing there," I said to Taylor. "Why don't they stop it?"

Several boat workers were determined to fight and singled out some of the more meek pacifists from the herd. As the fighting started, the workers cheered, and the singing stopped. It was a blood bath. I was powerless to do anything to stop this senseless violence, and I couldn't come to grips with it.

I looked toward where Taylor was, but he was gone.

The fighting swelled as the police just stood by, allowing the peaceful protesters to be beaten by the mob of yard workers. My eyes filled with tears as more angry yard workers joined the fight to get their licks in. Sticks, fists, and beer bottles flew through the air.

Finally, the police line moved forward. The police dragged the brutally injured pacifists by their ponytails. They tossed them in the prisoner vans without regard for their safety. Just a few workers were arrested, but they were escorted to squad cars.

My eyes were drawn to a young pacifist carrying a baby on her back. About a dozen yard workers started moving in toward her. She was in danger, and I felt I had to help her, so I ran as fast as possible down the parking lot stairs. By the time I reached her, she was on her knees shielding her baby. The only thing I could think to do was to identify as an electric boat employee. I squeezed between them and stood by her side and waved my employee badge for all of them to see. It worked, giving me the moment to whisk her off the street to safety.

The workers cheered the police and began to disperse as the prisoner vans were filled with as many protesters as they could hold.

Because of the violence they permitted, I lost respect for the police that day. I felt anger at the yard workers for their predisposition to fighting and bigotry. Most of all, I felt anguish because I did nothing more. Taylor was right. Violence ruled.

Office personnel returned to work but continued to chatter about the protesters and the launching of a submarine scheduled for later that day. Even in my department, George and Tom traded comments more loudly than usual.

"Did you see those commie pinkos run?" said George.

"Yeah. We should be allowed to shoot them and put them out of their misery," Tom added.

"I don't think they are communists," I responded.

Tom and George looked around at me, and I knew I was now in for an argument. But before it could start, the Department Chief shouted at the top of his lungs.

"Jones, Drexler, Sipe, Harris, and Gibson, get your asses in my office. Now."

It was like getting called to the principal's office for a disciplinary action. I didn't know any of the others called.

"What did you do now, wonder boy?" asked George.

"Maybe they're going to shoot you and put you out of your misery," added Tom.

I immediately headed for the Chief's office. When the five of us were assembled and sitting in his office, Randall Quantro came rushing in.

He sat on the edge of his desk and took a breath. "I'm going to make this short and sweet."

I quickly glanced around the group. They were as young and probably as inexperienced as me. Quantro waited until it was quiet enough to hear a pin drop.

"You have been selected for special duty - a mission," he started. "This is a voluntary assignment. Starting tomorrow...er Monday, you will no longer report to your workstation. Do not talk to anyone. I repeat, not to anyone. Not even to your union rep." He eyeballed each one of us.

"You are to punch in and go directly to the Navy complex, room 103. You will be there every day for the next several weeks. Any questions?"

After all I had seen at lunch, I had a general uneasiness about this special mission, my job, the company, and even my home life. My restlessness was a sense that I was not in control, perhaps in over my head, and in for more than I bargained.

At the same time, I was excited at the possibility of an adventure instead of my regular job. The rest of the group was all in. There weren't any questions, and chief Quantro asked one final question.

"Do each of you accept this assignment?"

We all nodded affirmatively, indicating that none of the group had any reservations.

"If you change your mind over the weekend," said Quantro, "go back to your job as usual, and don't talk to anyone about this conversation because it never happened. Okay, punch out and get the fuck out of here."

I stuck around for the launching of the Will Rogers submarine after being released from meeting with Quantro. Still, I made sure to stay clear of others in the nuclear design section so as not to be asked any questions about the meeting.

A special ceremonial party for the launching included various company dignitaries, local politicians, and Muriel Buck Humphrey, wife of the United States Vice President. She stood on a patriotically decorated platform against the flag-draped bow of the submarine. The submarine seemed huge, out of the water, resting on wooden pilings in the downhill launch alley leading to the river. The immensity of a submarine goes relatively unnoticed when it's in the water. Only the observation deck and part of the deck's surface are visible, then. I reflected on my confrontation with a sub while sailboating when I first arrived in New London. Now, standing in front of the bow of this new submarine, I realized the enormity of what was beneath me back then.

A great deal of political pageantry was included with this launching. It included band music and dignitaries giving hoopla speeches about the significance of the Polaris fleet. The prevailing belief was that an entire fleet of these attack submarines made us militarily superior and capable of destroying any nuclear aggression by any other world power. The theory at the time was that leaders of nations were sane and rational people who would never dare to start a war that would end in destroying their own country.

There was a huge applause as Mrs. Humphrey finally received the signal to break the traditional bottle of champagne on the bow. The first strike was feeble, and it rolled off the bow and dangled on the rope tied to it from the platform's railing. The President of Electric Boat retrieved the unbroken bottle and assisted her with the second and harder blow. Champagne splattered in all directions, and the yard horns blasted loudly. The overpowering flag-draped bow of the sub began to move toward the water. Yard workers threw their hard hats into the air, and the estimated crowd of thousands shouted, raised arms, and waved. The band played marching music as the submarine slid down the ramp into the river, creating a huge wave.

At this time, an unexpected event occurred. Out of nowhere, several rowboats appeared loaded with Hare Krishnas heading for the submarine. They tried to climb aboard the slippery round hull. The Navy personnel appeared confused about what to do. They decided not to shoot them in front of the dignitaries, which they had the right to do. They took oars and pushed those successfully climbing on top of the submarine back into the water. Other sailors used oars and pushed the rowboats away to prevent more from coming aboard. I didn't understand what the Krishnas intended to accomplish by this. But many yard workers laughed, jeered, and shouted for the Navy aboard to shoot them.

Several tugboats were positioned in the water to prevent the submarine from drifting into the muddy shore on the far side of the river and to tow the powerless submarine back to its berthing dock. It would take up to two years to be loaded with electronic equipment, weaponry, and missiles.

I left bewildered and mixed up emotionally about the entire day's events. I was thankful that the Navy chose not to shoot any of them. A small part of me was proud of our successful launch because it validated our work as shipbuilders. I wanted to believe that these superior lethal weapons made us unchallengeable in the world. Still, what Taylor said about the cost of peace and the cost of war made me rethink my position on war.

I was home early and therefore was the first to look at the mail that day. There was a letter from New Mexico State University. Without opening it, I stuffed it in my pocket alongside the Hare Krishna leaflet one of the protesters handed me before the launching. I got back into my VW and drove to the beach, where I sat on a big rock overlooking the sound. The pamphlet explained that the Krishnas were a distinctly Hindu religious sect. The pamphlet's content was difficult to understand; something about the soul being spiritually asleep and needing to be awakened to spiritual reality and connected with God.

Opening the letter from New Mexico State University, I remembered that I had applied to admissions just before taking the job with General Dynamics. This letter informed me that I was accepted as a graduate student and that upon arrival and evaluation was free to select an appropriate course of study. I was ecstatic about my acceptance. There were other attached forms to fill out concerning financing, housing, and health. I was too overjoyed with the opportunity to be concerned with the mountain of paperwork then.

I calmed down slowly after the horrendous events of that day by watching the boats coming in from the sound for a while and began grappling with the thought of going back to school. I hadn't given the idea much thought after applying many months earlier. My reasons for applying to a New Mexico university came back to me. I remembered a car trip with four other Boy Scouts to Philmont Scout Ranch in Cimarron, New Mexico. A hike through the wilderness ranch, ascending from the prairie desert scrub at 3,000 feet through rough mountainous terrain to the Baldy Mountain peak at 12,500 feet, left me with an unforgettable memory of the Southwest. The desert fascinated me, and now I was presented with the opportunity to live there.

A small diesel submarine came chugging up the river, and my thoughts turned back to the events that happened that day. Most prevalent was Taylor's opposing view of the military industry. It added fuel to my growing disillusionment with the whole defense mindset.

I realized that the speeches at the launching told us what we all wanted to hear or what we wanted to believe about being the top dog militarily. The speakers at the launching proclaimed that tyrants will always find places in the world to rule. Surely, as nuclear technology spread, unreasoning powers would make unrealistic commitments to developing more sophisticated weaponry. Not that our authorities were not doing the same at the taxpayer's expense. The whole concept of nuclear deterrence was based on our government's assumption that insane people would never become heads of state in the first place. So, there wouldn't be any leaders to start a nuclear war when faced with the assurance that their nation was about to be destroyed. Contrary to that belief, there have been and will continue to be some senseless leaders with hard- nosed illusions of grandeur. But I had doubts that bigger guns would frighten any country into a submissive peace for very long.

My ongoing training for the special mission wasn't near completion as far as I knew. It was exciting because there were only five of us, which meant it was possibly important. Since no mission was scheduled yet, I figured that I had some time to think.

I had a decision to make. A fork in the road lay before me, and I had to decide what I wanted to do for myself. I thought I would take my time to make the decision, but I realized I had already made it. We were going to New Mexico!

On my way home, I thought about my relationship with Ginny. It was becoming strained due to a lack of communication between us. My instinct was to wait for the appropriate moment, not knowing if I could recognize it when it came. Besides, I needed to complete the other forms in the packet that came with the acceptance letter.

Chapter 15
THE DAY MY LIFE STARTED COMING APART

Going past Harry on my way to the Navy complex, several designers crowded near the windows overlooking the yard. Ijoined them to see what was going on. Nuclear missiles were being loaded onto the USS Sturgeon, scheduled to be commissioned in March of 1967. The long slender white cylinders were being lowered by crane into the open hatches of the missile silos. I counted sixteen hatches, and as I did, a strange and disconcerting feeling sickened me. Up until now, I felt I was part of something important. Very important. Much bigger than me. The images of the missiles burned into my brain forever at that moment. They would never leave me.

Behind me, several guys boastfully talked about how many people would die in the first 10 seconds, in 20 seconds, and in the first minute if one of the lethal weapons were to hit New York City. They talked about the horrid estimate of destruction with an exuberance of superiority about an indiscriminate mass killing of a colossal number of innocent people. The missiles were a force not focused directly on the enemy, and they were singing their own praises that we were the top dog by sheer numbers of nuclear warheads.

Suddenly, I was startled when a hand was laid on my shoulder. It was Harry.

"What are you doing here?"

"I'm on my way to, ah, to the yard," I replied.

"I know where you're supposed to be, and it's important that you get there on time."

Harry knew about everything that was going on. He knew where I was going. Did he know about the mission I was on? He knew everybody's business, even personal business. He was familiar with the apartment complex where I lived. He asked me if I needed help buying furniture and gave me a contact that he said would be honest with me and that I could trust him.

"Just tell him how much you want to spend, and he will put a package together for you."

Harry's contact put the package together, and I bought a living room and dining room set.

Everyone always trusted Harry. He had such an authoritative and trustworthy demeanor. I always wondered who his sources of information were, but I never questioned him, and no one would.

I reported to the Navy office, room 103, instead of going to the Nuclear Design Department. The other four guys chosen for this special assignment were there too. We were each assigned to our own long table by a Navy officer sitting at a tiny desk in the front of the room. He was dressed in traditional white but had no identification or sign of rank and never volunteered any personal information. On each table was a stack of plans at one end. Next to the stack was a writing tablet and a stack of pencils.

"When I tell you to begin," the Navy man barked in a baritone voice, "grab a plan from the pile on your table and memorize as much as possible until you hear the timer go off. Then I will ask some questions to determine how much you have learned."

Over and over again, we took a plan, studied it, and answered questions from the Navy officer. The questions were very general. Approximately how long was the plan? What was the subject matter?

What particular items were addressed in the plan? This went on for the entire day except for a small lunch break at the food trucks parked directly outside. We were not to socialize with our fellow workers.

Several weeks went by while we continued to do this work. Every time the stacks of drawings dwindled, more were added. The exercise would have been arduous except that the nature of the questions became more system oriented rather than just items. I had never seen submarine structural drawings or compartment layouts before. We were learning a lot and seeing more than we ever would working at our specific individual jobs.

One day when we reported to room 103, we unexpectedly found a note taped to the door. It read, "There will be no further testing. Each of you has met the goals of this class. Congratulations. Today you are to immediately report to your Department Chief without ever discussing your training with each other or with anyone."

We all assembled in Chief Quantro's office. He came storming in within moments and slammed the door behind him. Then, picking up a small stack of papers, he handed a sheet to each one of us.

"Each of you has been chosen to go on a mission. Without any further details for now, tomorrow you are to return to your jobs until further notice. You are not to talk to anyone about your training for this mission. Use the need-to-know policy if you have to. This is a list of items that you are to put in a duffle bag," he continued. "Keep the duffel bag as near as possible to your front door. Sometime in the near future, you will receive a telephone call. It could be any time of the day or night. This person will tell you something about yourself that only you know, so you can be assured that you are talking to an authorized contact. Follow the contact's instructions without question. Have your wife or girlfriend take you to the designated drop-off. Say your goodbyes and wait there alone. When your contact arrives, he will once again tell you something about yourself that only you know. Go with him and follow his instructions. You will not return home for about three months."

It was now or never, a decision had to be made whether to leave EB or go on the secretive mission. Should I take advantage of the opportunity of the war machine or hope for excitement and adventure by going back to school? Could I live with the consequences of my choice?

I drove to my favorite spot on the New London shore and made my way out on the breaker that protects the shoreline from large waves by jumping from rock to rock. I sat on a large rock and I considered all the reasons why I should go back to school. At the same time, my thoughts about staying challenged these feelings. The pay was fabulous. Even considering for the moment that military superiority deterred war, I just couldn't whitewash the dirty feeling and excuse what I was doing as being patriotic. Try as I did to find a reason to stay, I just couldn't support the effort to increase military power as the only way toward world peace. I felt I had compromised my morals.

Now it was time to tell Ginny about the fork in the road of my life and my desire to leave Connecticut for the "Land of Enchantment," as the state slogan for New Mexico says. I laid out the details as best I could about the adventure upon which we were about to embark. Pending a credit review by the university administration, I could transfer enough credits to start my graduate courses right away while simultaneously having to make up for any undergraduate deficiencies.

I painted a pretty picture of what New Mexico was like from a few pictures included in the information package. I showed her an architectural concept drawing of the marital housing on campus that was currently under construction. She knew from my excitement that I would take advantage of the opportunity and listened carefully but mainly remained silent. Her silence led me to believe she was reluctant but was willing to go with my decision.

I hadn't been with Electric Boat very long, so I figured the company wouldn't have much to say about my quitting. I soon found out that was not the case once I informed my supervisor, Fishface, that I was leaving.

"I've only been working here for a year, so I think a week's notice is fair, right?"

"That's not up to me, or you for that matter," he responded without making eye contact. He headed for his phone within seconds of finishing our short conversation.

George and Tom turned around upon the supervisor leaving the immediate area. "Did I hear you right, college boy? You're leaving us miserable low lifers?" asked George.

"Yeah? You had enough of us?" added Tom.

"I have an opportunity to go back to college, and I think I should take it," I said.

"Where's this institution of higher learning?" asked George sarcastically.

"New Mexico," I replied.

"They have colleges out there?" questioned George. "I always thought New Mexico was nothing but desert and rattlesnakes."

"Yeah, and wild Indians," added Tom.

I tried to think of a clever response, but only seconds passed when three FBI men in black suits came up to me.

"Stop what you are doing and come with us," one of them said.

I didn't expect to be arrested. I empathized with how humiliating it must have been for Taylor, our fellow drunk designer, when he was arrested. I started to put my things away.

"Never mind that now," spoke the same agent.

I felt like the eyes of everybody in the entire nuclear design department were watching me being marched down the long isle and eventually through the doors into the stairwell.

"Why so serious? Did I do something wrong?" I questioned.

There was no reply, only the sound of our shoes echoing off the staircase steps as we descended two floors, then through doors and into a little ten-by-ten interior room. The room was bare except for one chair in the middle.

"Sit," snarled the agent.

As I did, another agent went for the light switch and lowered the lighting of the room, and then turned on a single light centered on my face. This made it impossible to distinguish their faces among the shadows, just like in the old black-and-white detective movies. They rapidly started firing questions.

"Why have you decided to leave Electric Boat? Why are you going there? Do you know anyone there?"

I tried to answer the questions as rapidly as they asked them. My sentences were not even finished before they would ask another one.

The petty questions went on and on for quite a time. Then I heard the door to the room open, and I saw the silhouettes of several other people enter the room closing the door behind them. The questions suddenly changed. They became more specific.

"Where did you live while you were a student at Point Park College?"

"In the dormitory," I replied.

"The whole time?"

"No. I moved into a house my last year."

"Why?"

"Because it was too expensive to live in the dorms."

"Where was the house located? Why that house?"

"An acquaintance at school told me about it. He already had a room there."

"Who was this acquaintance? How well did you know him?"

"Frank, Frank Palumbo. I didn't know him all that well. He came from Altoona."

"How many boarders lived in that house?"

"Eight, I believe."

"What are their names?"

"I don't remember. We were all students. Five of them were going to PIMS."

"PIMS?"

"Pittsburgh Institute of Mortuary Science. They were all going to be morticians. That's why I didn't know them. I didn't really want to associate with them."

"And the others?"

"Frank attended Point Park, and another lived in the basement. He was a medical student at Pitt. His name was Bob, I think."

"Why didn't you tell us about living there on your application for employment?"

"I didn't think it was important at the time. Besides, I didn't even live there a year."

"Who owned the house?"

"Some old woman. A foreigner."

"Did you ever have a conversation with her?"

"Not really."

"What do you mean?"

"She was difficult to understand."

"What did you talk about?"

"She hired a contractor to re-plaster her dining room. I had never seen plastering over wood lath, so I asked her if it would be okay to watch him work."

"That was it?"

"Yes."

"Why did you want to watch the work being done?"

"I was an engineering student with a major in mechanical and a minor in architectural design. I was curious."

"How did you pay rent?"

"I made out a check and gave it to one of the PIMS students. His name was Marty, I think."

"Who did you make it out to?"

"I left that blank as Marty instructed me to."

"What name was on the cancelled check?"

"Marty's name."

"You didn't think that was strange?"

"Look, I didn't care. The rent was 35 dollars a month. Marty gave me written receipts, so I didn't care what he did with the check."

"The lady that owned the house was a Russian. We ask you one more time, are you sure you never talked to her any other time?"

"I'm sure."

Suddenly the lights in the room were turned on. I was blinded for a few seconds. All I wanted to do was get out of there. I wanted to get away from submarines and the war business as soon as possible.

"Are you aware that your level of security has been raised to Top Secret?"

"No, really? I didn't apply for it."

"It was approved when you started training for your upcoming mission."

"I didn't know. How can you do that without asking me?"

"Do you have a problem with it?"

"No. In fact, I'm flattered. I thought I was being arrested."

"In light of your classification change, would you like to withdraw your resignation?"

Chapter 16
TIME FOR A CAREER CHANGE

My sailboat sold right away. I was sorry to see it go, but it would never be used in the desert.

I rented the 18-foot U-Haul truck and backed it up against the slight hill that ascended to the edge of the rear parking lot of my apartment building. This made the truck's bed low enough for me to drive the VW from the parking lot into the truck and to one side. Ginny helped me load what little furniture we owned. We first took the drawers and cushions out and stacked them beside the truck. We started with putting the mattress on the car and other clothing items we wouldn't need for the trip. The other furniture fit next to and behind the car at the truck's rear. The drawers and cushions served as buffers for everything else we squeezed in. By the time we were done packing, the truck was filled, and we were off to her parent's home in Pennsylvania.

We crept quietly into Ginny's unfurnished room and went to Sleep on the floor without her parents knowing. The next morning, we surprised her mother at the breakfast table. Shortly after that, Earl came toward the kitchen, stopped, and noticed the U-Haul truck out front.

"Somebody moving? There's a moving truck parked out front." He turned and noticed us at the table. "Well! Well! Did you decide to come work for the family, Weldon?"

"No, not exactly," I replied. "I'm not ready for the paving business." As usual, he took offense to everything I said.

"Hey, don't knock it, young man," he rebuked my reply. "The streets really are lined with gold. It pays for all this," he declared with a wide-reaching wave of his arm.

Then he cut a bite of meat from a slice of ham Dorothy had put on his plate and began chewing it without closing his mouth and pointing his fork at me.

"You know, son, I've paid my dues, and you've got to pay yours. They will take it away from you if you don't get yours with hard work and perseverance. No one's going to give you what you don't earn--or can't screw them out of!"

Dorothy gasped.

Because Earl was already wound up from our unexpected visit, I figured I might as well jump in with both feet and defend myself.

"I've been accepted for graduate study."

"Ah! Not more God damn college," he rebutted, "This world doesn't need any more philosophers."

He was continually disappointed with my decisions.

"No, actually, I'm going to study political science," was my smart- ass reply.

He tried to digest the conversation for a moment. Then his look of disgust was replaced by one of mild resignation and a long exhale.

"Political Science, eh?"

He hesitated until he formulated a comeback.

"Well, I guess you can make some money being a politician. I ought to know. I've paid off over half of them chumps to build this business into the largest road construction company in the state.”

I tried to keep the conversation on point.

“We’re moving to New Mexico.”

“Out of the country?” responded Dorothy in alarm. “Why you don’t even speak the language!”

“No. New Mexico, Mother,” said Ginny. “It’s in the United States ...somewhere ...in the desert. I think they speak English there. Don’t they Weldon?”

“In the desert?” retorted Earl. “There’s nothing there, for Christ’s sake, except rattlesnakes and drunken Indians. No, you’re not taking my daughter away from all this while you go philosophize in the desert.”

The conversation went on a little longer, but Ginny stood by my decision to go, though there was still some reluctance in her voice. At the time, I figured her additional lack of enthusiasm was due to her mother’s sadness about us leaving.

Chapter 17
WESTWARD HO

LIKE A ROLLING STONE – Bob Dylan

Once upon a time you dressed so fine

Threw the bums a dime in your prime, didn't you?

People call say 'beware doll, you're bound to fall'

You thought they were all kidding you

You used to laugh about

Everybody that was hanging out

Now you don't talk so loud

Now you don't seem so proud

About having to be scrounging your next meal

How does it feel, how does it feel?

To be without a home

Like a complete unknown, like a rolling stone

Ahh you've gone to the finest schools, alright Miss Lonely

But you know you only used to get juiced in it

Nobody's ever taught you how to live out on the street

And now you're gonna have to get used to it

You say you never compromise

With the mystery tramp, but now you realize

He's not selling any alibis

As you stare into the vacuum of his eyes

And say do you want to make a deal?

How does it feel, how does it feel?

To be on your own, with no direction home

A complete unknown, like a rolling stone

Ahh princess on a steeple and all the pretty people

They're all drinking, thinking that they've got it made
Exchanging all precious gifts
But you better take your diamond ring, you better pawn it
babe
You used to be so amused

At Napoleon in rags and the language that he used
Go to him he calls you, you can't refuse

When you ain't got nothing, you got nothing to lose
You're invisible now, you've got no secrets to conceal
How does it feel, ah how does it feel?

To be on your own, with no direction home
Like a complete unknown, like a rolling stone

...

Driving across the country in a U-Haul truck was a
grueling ordeal. The air conditioning worked okay at first,
but the more west we traveled, the less efficient it became.
We started opening the windows in the morning and in the
early evening because the wind's tornado-like conditions
made the heat in the cab more bearable. One consequence
of the wind was that it made it very noisy. The cab was
already noisy from the diesel engine. Still, it was much
louder with the windows opened, making it impossible to
have detailed conversations.

Our conversations were short with the cyclone effect in the
cab.

"Hungry?"

"Rest stop?"

"Gas?"

On the other side of St. Louis, the roads straightened
out. Speed limits increased to at least 70 mph, but I couldn't
go faster than 50 mph due to the extra weight of the VW.

Our speed limit might have reached as high as 60 mph if we were going downhill and had no headwind.

With every mile farther away from submarines, I became more at peace. I realized that the little bit of pride related to the job at Electric Boat was replaced with guilt about the production of weapons of mass destruction.

The open highway meant freedom for me. It was exhilarating having no home to go to, no family ties, and what lay ahead was completely unknown. We stayed in cheap motels. Several nights just napped in the cab at a truck stop. We ate hamburgers and hotdogs at dives and drive-ins to conserve our money. What an adventure for me!

For Ginny, it was a regretful experience. However, I wasn't aware of it at the time. She became less talkative, which I thought was because the truck was hot, noisy, and uncomfortable. Actually, she was becoming withdrawn. With every mile away from home, her comfort as a pampered girl was replaced with the realization that she would no longer be treated like a rich girl. Being on her own meant she was essentially duty-bound to me. Perhaps this was when she started to feel I wasn't where her happiness lay. We had nothing but what was in the truck and the cash that was in my pocket. I drove onward, feeling euphoric that I had nothing to lose.

The sun beat down brighter the more west we drove. The skies were clear, and the daylight lasted past nine o'clock in the evening. Some days we were on the road by 5 a.m., and the sun was already up when we awoke. On those mornings, we stopped for breakfast when the traffic got busy. Breakfast was our biggest meal and the most appreciated. The food improved the farther we drove, and the prices were lower than back east.

The terrain of the Blue Ridge Mountains and dirty old industrial towns like Wheeling and Saint Louis gave way to seemingly never- ending fields of corn and wheat after crossing the mighty disappointing Mississippi River.

By the time we reached the plains of Oklahoma and the flat nothingness of the Texas panhandle, we were both thoroughly windblown. Our eyes started to adjust to the sun, but the squinting continued as desert sand mixed in with the open-window breeze.

Finally, we crossed the Texas border into New Mexico. We stopped and took a picture of the "Welcome to New Mexico, Land of Enchantment." sign with an Instamatic camera. The terrain was improved a little from where we had been. Still, we decided to get off the Interstate and take route 54, which angles southward toward Alamogordo, New Mexico.

This final part of our trip was indeed enchanting. El Malpais (or Bad Lands in English) was a mysterious landscape with sandstone bluffs, jagged peaks, and open grassland valleys. Turning onto route 70 had further surprises. The Capitan Mountains, followed by the Lincoln National Forest, were off to our left. To our right, it looked like snow. It was the White Sands National Monument, a natural dune field of gypsum remaining from an ancient seabed that was once there. The dunes came close to the highway after a while. Off to the left was a line of colossal radio frequency dishes aimed toward the sky. To the right was an entrance road with a sign indicating it was to the NASA Manned Spacecraft Center – White Sands Test Facility. The test facility performed around-the-clock tests of the propulsion systems of the Apollo Command Module and the Lunar Landing Module in preparation for our astronauts' first landing on the moon.

We passed the sand dunes within a few miles, and ahead of us were the looming Organ Mountains that resembled a church organ's pipes. We started a steep ascent through the Organ pass, then our rapid descent down onto the flat desert below.

Las Cruces was a one-horse town. We thought we were lost as only a few buildings were in sight, so we stopped for gas and directions to the university. The directions were simple.

"Keep driving," said the station attendant, "you'll run into it."

He was right. There was nothing but desert until suddenly there it was, a cluster of buildings like an oasis. We followed the directions through the campus to where we were to stay temporarily until the ongoing construction of the new married housing was completed. It looked as though it was almost finished when we drove by. A sign read

'BRACEWELL VILLAGE:

MARRIED STUDENT HOUSING.'

Someone had drawn a line through the last three words and written 'COMMUNE' above it.

The directions led us to what could be considered a slum in the inner city. Two streets of barracks were in poor shape and needed to be torn down, and no exteriors had been painted for years. The barren streets and driveways were unpaved dirt paths, indistinguishable from some small areas that were past attempts to grow grass for front lawns. Many screen doors and windows needed repair, and some doors were left open without concern for theft.

"Are you sure we followed the directions?" asked Ginny. I read them again to make sure and got out of the truck in disbelief. I didn't see anyone else, so I picked a barracks that seemed somewhat habitable and went inside. The screen door came off its hinges when I opened it. Inside was a bleak living room with only several pieces of stuffed lounge furniture left behind, a dead lizard, and some flies. A thick layer of desert sand covered everything.

Ginny wouldn't get out of the truck at first, but after I signaled her to come, she got out but leaned against the truck, refusing to go any further.

Just then, a couple came out from another barracks building several doors down. They headed straight for us as we stood next to the truck. The guy was tall, well-built, and blond-haired. His female companion was shorter, buxom, and had over-the-shoulder blond hair.

"Are ya lost?" said the young woman with a strong western twang.

"I hope so," Ginny responded with negativity. "Surely this can't be the married student housing?"

"I'm afraid it is," said the young man with his slow western twang. He seemed a little reserved but guessed right away we weren't locals.

"We were thinking the same thing when we moved in, but this is it all right," said the woman trying to comfort Ginny.

The young man seemed to get taller as he got closer. He quickly extended his hand in friendship.

"Jim Spring. This is ma wife, Glenda."

"Howdy," added Glenda.

Ginny wanted to get to the point with me about staying there. "No offense but Weldon, this is a dump."

She was so frank that she embarrassed me. "Gin, it's all there is until marital housing opens up."

"It's not much, I'll grant ya that, but it'll do," said Jim coming to my rescue. "Electric is okay. Plumbing too. Swamp coolers need fixin ..."

"Swamp coolers?" I asked.

"Air conditioners," he responded, then seeing that I didn't understand, "Evaporative coolers."

I hesitated enough that he figured I still didn't know what evaporative coolers were. "Guess you easterners wouldn't know about them. Air is sucked through straw pads with water running over them. Kind-da-like a wet towel on your face in the breeze."

"Swamp coolers," I repeated in astonishment."

"They work pretty good when the temperature gets over a hundred," snapped Jim.

"How high does the temperature get here, anyway?" I asked unknowingly.

"About a hundred and twenty ..." then with a slight smile, "in the shade!"

There was something about Jim that made me like him. Little did I know then he would become a close friend.

I extended my hand. "Weldon Sipe and this is my wife, Ginny."

As the day went on, other students showed up with pickups and various makeshift vehicles filled with furniture, clothes, and personal things. Most of the vehicles had New Mexico license plates which I assumed meant they were state residents.

Jim and Glenda helped Ginny and me unload the truck, except for the VW. They were amazed that the car was in the truck.

"How'd you figure on getting the car out of there?"Jim asked.

"I really hadn't figured out how," was my response, and I continued explaining how I had got it in there in the first place.

"It's pretty flat around these parts. We could drive around all day and not find a suitable hill to back it up to," said Jim

"How about a railroad? Is there one in Las Cruces," I asked.

Jim went to his pick-up truck parked behind his barrack and returned shortly with a road map of Las Cruces. Sure enough, there was one on the map, marked with a flag indicating no passenger service and probably abandoned.

We located the station in an arid desert area on the edge of town. There was only a small building with a wooden loading platform that seemed about the right height for the truck bed. We backed the truck up to the platform, which left about a foot gap to the truck bed. I was worried that the car tires would get stuck in the gap, and I would be in quite a fix. As luck would have it, Jim found several steel plates just the right length to cover the gap between the truck and the platform. We barely managed to move them into place, and I backed the VW out of the truck and drove down the ramp of the loading platform into the desert sand.

We stopped at a liquor store in Las Cruces before heading toward University Park. At Jim's suggestion, I treated us to a six-pack of Coors because it was the most popular local beer.

Chapter 18

THE LAND OF MAÑANA

Registration day in the cafeteria was laid back but still confusing. Lines of students everywhere filled the place. The day's objective was to collect keypunch cards for the classes you wanted to take. This was done on the first day of registration. Once all the cards for a class had been passed out, the class was considered closed for the semester. The teachers managed the class tables where the key-punch cards were handed out. They were uncaring and bureaucratic.

I made it through each class table and managed to get keypunch cards for each class that the administration suggested I take. At the final approval table, I listened to an ongoing conversation between a student named Tommy and an Advisor. Tommy was a little short, thin guy and a pipe smoker.

"I don't see any ROTC on here," said the Advisor to Tommy. "Everyone's required to take ROTC here to graduate."

That was true, I thought. I remembered something about it being a Spanish land grant college; therefore, military training was required. I quickly learned that most students didn't know they had to take ROTC. This was distressing, with the Vietnam conflict being front page news daily. Your draft board knew about your military training upon graduation. This meant you should expect an Army Recruiter to appear quickly on your doorstep.

"Yeah, well, I'm a transfer student," said Tommy. "From where?" snapped the Advisor.

"Carlsbad Community College," responded Tommy.

"Degreed?" "Yeah."

The advisor had a large records book in front of him to spot- check information he was being given by students. Still, it became evident to me during the day that most of the Advisors were quick to accept any excuse as to why a student wasn't enrolled in ROTC. Further, they ignored that many students slid past the ROTC table to avoid the subject entirely.

"OK. Next," said the Advisor as he motioned for Tommy to get out of his face.

Tommy stepped to the next advisor at the table. The advisor reached for my keypunch cards as I was next in line. I handed them to him.

"I don't see any ROTC on here," said the Advisor. "Everyone's required to ...."

"I'm a transfer student," I interrupted. Tommy looked over at me with interest. "From Point Park College," I added. "Degreed?"

"Yes," I snapped.

The Advisor grabbed one of his big binders and started looking for Point Park College.

"I never heard of Point Park College," he muttered sarcastically.

Within a few moments, it became too laborious for him to bother to check it out. He really didn't care.

"How many credits did you transfer?"

I was trying to remember how many credits I had actually earned when I noticed a sign on his table saying, "Students with less than 72 transferred credits must take ROTC."

That meant I had to say something larger than 72, so I made my answer " 138. I earned 138 credits."

After some hesitance, the Advisor looked past me to the next student in line.

"Next," he said, reaching around me for the class cards of the student behind me.

I quickly walked away while the getting was good.

Tommy caught up with me outside of the cafeteria. "Hey man, do you really have a degree?"

"Yeah," I said, "but they didn't accept more than 38 hours cause I'm switching majors," I replied.

"Pretty smart," Tommy said. "They're so busy they'll never catch it. What's your major?"

"Political Science," I replied.

"Same here," he said as he extended his hand. "I'm Tommy Yancy, by the way."

"Weldon Sipe," I said.

"What kind of name is that?"

We continued walking together as we exchanged more background information and headed toward the student housing office. He also hoped to get into the housing development as soon as possible. We were both surprised that we could move into one of the newly completed complexes and were assigned neighboring condos.

"Well, I guess we are neighbors," he said as we left the housing office.

"Guess we are," I replied with a smile.

We walked across the ROTC parade ground in front of Hadley Hall, which served as the Administration building. There we paid for tuition fees and any extra services like lab fees. In front of Hadley Hall was a large, bricked patio area with many mingling students and sign- up tables, banners, and signs. Fraternities, Sororities, and many clubs like the 4H and even church youth organizations were present.

"What's all this?" I asked Tommy

"This is the free speech area."

Not knowing what he meant, I questioned him, "Free speech?"

"Students hand out leaflets to join clubs and social groups, and collect money for political causes, or get signatures for a petition, that sort of thing. It's a tradition that this area is for nontraditional activities not allowed elsewhere on campus."

Tommy noticed a familiar face among the crowd.

"There's Benny. He's one of the most politically active students on campus. He lives for politics ever since he got out of the army. He was in engineering last semester, but he's transferring to Political Science. Come on, I'll introduce you."

We made our way to the SDS organization table, where Benny was giving a spiel about the Students for a Democratic Society. He was a barrel-built militant who talked persuasively about the SDS agenda to a student. As he talked, it was noticeable that he had a stutter, and occasionally it seemed to get the best of him.

"The SDS started at the University of Michigan in 1960. They started out principally involved in civil rights; however, they continued the anti-war effort following their successful na-na-national ...here, read their Port Huron Statement."

Benny attempted to hand him a copy, but the student brushed it aside. "Frankly, we ought to just kill you yella bastards!"

Benny stood his ground, pinched his nostrils closed, and made the sound of a quiz show buzzer.

"Aaaaaaa ... Wrong answer!"

Taking note of Benny's size, the student decided to back away and walked off.

"If I'm yellow," said Benny, "then why are you the one walking away?"

Benny's attempt to taunt him to come back didn't work. Then he saw Tommy.

"Hey, Tommy! Que Pasa?"

"Nada," responded Tommy. "Nada damn thing. Benny, this here's Weldon Sipe, a Yankee from back East. Weldon, Joe Benedict. We call him Benny."

"Yankee, eh? Good! The scales are tipped in favor of the Okies around here."

I picked up a copy of the Port Huron Statement to read later when suddenly, with a loud thump, some man in dress shoes was on the table right in front of my face.

Benny looked up with surprise. "Just when I was on a roll," he commented.

It was the Assistant Dean. "The school has issued notices that these activities aren't going to be permitted anymore. If you don't take these tables down, you'll be cited."

"Oh, here we go again," said Benny going from being surprised to pissed off. "Just wh-wh-what student activities are you referring to this time?"

"There will be no fundraising and no promoting political causes on campus," he stated prophetically.

"You can't urge a particular issue, you can't raise money, you can't hold a rally here, and you can't incite a protest or demonstration anywhere on or off campus, and you can't give speeches. All this is prohibited from now on."

"So why didn't you just say that there is no free speech in the free speech area? Th-th-that's inclusive of just about everything we do here."

"I guess it is, isn't it," retorted the Assistant Dean as he jumped down from the table. "Come on now. Get these tables down."

He walked back to the administration building. Slowly, the disgruntled students began taking the tables down once the Assistant Dean disappeared into Hadley Hall.

"Well, I guess that's it for today," Benny said.

"Today?" I said.

"This is an ongoing routine with the Administration, and we will all be back at it in a few days." Benny saw that I was befuddled. "Tommy, bring Weldon to the next SDS meeting so we can get him up to speed."

"That's a good idea," said Tommy.

"It's all in the Port Huron Statement," said Benny pointing the copy in my hand. "That's the official position of the SDS. Come to the me-me-meeting next Tuesday night. You'll find it quite colorful. Mostly average students with a few radicals ones here and there."

Tommy and I walked to Bracewell Village. He told me how he had met Benny at a campus orientation meeting and had already been to one meeting of the Students for a Democratic Society.

Chapter 19
SETTLING IN

Over the next several days, we moved into our new apartment. Tommy and I helped each other move the heavier things. Tommy's wife, Susan, and Ginny got along well. Susan was an LPN and worked days, meaning Ginny was at home alone most of the time.

I was anxious to read through the Port Huron Statement. Ginny made grinders for dinner, and I took mine into the living room, quietly sat down, cracked open the 72-page Port Huron paper, and started reading. After a few minutes, Ginny joined me in the living room. She started to watch our tiny tabletop TV that only had rabbit ear reception.

I barely read a few pages when she broke the sound barrier created by the TV noise and the swamp cooler's rumbling.

"Just what am I supposed to do while you're at school?"

I tried to ignore her at first, but she glared at me. "I don't know. Find something to do," I said. "Like what?" she retorted.

I was slightly perturbed that she interrupted my reading. "Get a job or something."

Now she was angry. "I didn't move to this God-forsaken sand dune you call a state to get a job."

We had had this conversation before, and I didn't want to repeat it, so I pretended to be engrossed in the report.

She quietly got up, shut off the TV, and climbed the stairs toward the bedroom.

The next day was the first day of Dr. Hadsell's Political Science class. Tommy and I were already sitting beside each other when Benny wandered over and joined us.

"Hey, Q-Q-Que Pasa boys," he said boisterously.

"Nada," replied Tommy. "Nada damn thing!"

Professor Hadsell came rushing in and added several more books to an already two-foot stack on his desk. He then sat on the other front corner of his small desk, close to the front row. He was a middle-aged man with a slender to average build and long, straight light brown hair, that he often had to brush away from his eyes. He had a bold, authoritative ego-driven personality though he never raised his voice.

He talked somewhat rushed, like he walked, almost as if he was making sure he wouldn't forget his discussion points.

"In this class, we will be questioning the social and ethical theories of the influential historical thinkers and master philosophers such as Plato, Aristotle, Rousseau, Hobbes, Bentham, Mill, and Locke," he started out. Already some students were taking notes. Benny was one of them.

He placed his hand reverently on the stack of books.

"I have chosen a selection of 35 textbooks from the Graduate Library for this course. There are plenty of copies in the library for takeout. Your final exam may be over one of these, some of these, all of these, or none of these."

Some students expressed negative sounds while he silently pulled a small tin can from the inside vest pocket of his camel corduroy jacket. He removed a small cigar, tapped it on the tin can, and then put it in his mouth. He delayed speaking while he searched several pockets for his lighter and lit the stubby thing. He took a drag and then began talking again.

"Your final exam may be over something we discuss in class, so it behooves you to be here, although I don't take attendance. I already have your money, so it doesn't matter to me if you attend. There is a signup sheet floating around, which you may sign if you feel the need to."

He took another drag on his cigar.

"Well, that's it for today. Class dismissed." And with that, he left the room.

As he did, several students shouted, "Study group," and began forming groups. I joined Tommy, Benny, Jim, and

Frankie, who introduced himself as another neighbor from Bracewell Village. We decided it would be better to adjourn to the Graduate Library, where copies of the referred books were located. The Graduate Library was limited to post-grad students' use only. Upon our first visit, we were issued keys to access it 24/7. Studying was convienient with access to free copy machines, typewriters, paper, office supplies, and telephones. During the day, there were free secretarial services as well.

Half of the room consisted of labeled shelves of books. The other half was an open area devoted to a large conference table, and individual lounge chairs here and there scattered around the room near windows or near floor lamps. We all sat around the conference table, introduced ourselves, and exchanged addresses and other background information. None of us had home telephones yet, and we were all on a waiting list for installations. Down the street near the entrance to the village was one telephone booth for all to use. Seemed there was always someone using it, especially on holidays.

I was getting to know Jim. He was new to the rest of the group and was a local boy from Clayton, a small town in the northeast part of the state. Frankie was from Massachusetts. His wife Mary was from there also and was already complaining about the desert and the heat, and I thought she and Ginny would hit it off on that basis alone. Already acquainted with Tommy, Benny told us why he decided to leave the Army. None of us understood what Benny was conveying about his departure. He said he was a Sergeant, Master Sergeant, or some such rank. He and his wife Judy lived on the next block down from us.

Soon we got down to the business at hand. "Thirty-five textbooks for one class!" remarked Jim. "Dang! I think he's trying to kill us."

"We don't have any ch-ch-choice," Benny added. "We have to do well because Political Science is our ma-major. We'll be seeing a lot of Dr. Hadsell."

Tommy puffed on his pipe. "Jim's right. We better make 'A's in this class, especially since it's a required survey course. He can make graduate school hell for us."

"Well, that's it then," said Benny with authority. "We'll divide up the books, five each, and we'll each outline our five an-and exchange one outline weekly."

"Except for what Hadsell chooses to talk about in class," I added. "We better swap notes the following day before class."

We took turns taking one off the top of the stack until they were gone.

Our apartment was dark when I got home, and I didn't turn on the kitchen light but found the refrigerator. Inside was a plate of food with clear wrap over it prepared for me. Ginny had already gone to bed. In a way, I was glad that she went to bed. That way, I avoided hearing how lonely she was or any other complaints. I was clueless and felt guilty because I didn't know what to do for her. I couldn't help her during the week and couldn't spend a lot of time with her on weekends unless my school load was light. I gobbled down the food and climbed the stairs.

I removed my clothes, letting everything fall to the floor, and crawled into bed. Ginny stirred a little.

"I stayed up as long as I could," she said with a yawn. Now I really felt guilty. I snuggled up against her. "Sorry honey, there's a lot of reading an...."

"Just go to sleep," she snapped. "You want some. You're going to have to get home earlier."

I felt disheartened that I wasn't being praised. Still, she had no idea what graduate school was like, or undergraduate college, either, for that matter. No one who hasn't been there knows what it's like, and there is no comparison to high school – not even to undergraduate college, really. So, I rolled over on my back and looked at the ceiling to calm down.

After trying to relax for what seemed a long time, I noticed a faint rhythmic rubbing sound coming through the wall. At first, I thought it was the sound of the swamp cooler rumbling away, but the rhythm wasn't steady. Sometimes it was fast, and other times slow.

"What the hell is that?" I said without giving thought to Ginny sleeping.

She stirred a little but didn't wake up or respond.

I was curious enough to get up and put my ear to the wall. The rhythmic rubbing got louder, but then it suddenly stopped. I listened a bit longer to see if it would start again, and it didn't, so I got back into bed.

"Sounds like somebody is sanding wood or something," I said aloud but not enough to disturb Ginny. "Who the hell would be making furniture late at night? That's a hell of a hobby."

Chapter 20
THE CLASS ROUTINE

It was the first lecture day of Dr. Hadsell's Political Science class. It was hot, and we were all roasting. This class was held in an old wooden barracks building, a temporary classroom until construction was completed on several new classroom buildings. The few windows were open just enough to circulate some of the air from a single swamp cooler that didn't cool much and occasionally dripped water on the linoleum floor. Hadsell spoke in a monotone voice but was loud enough to be heard over the swamp cooler.

My study group sat together. We were somewhat interested in the introductory material. Benny stayed focused and was the only one in the class taking notes. The non-political science majors were bored. They only took this class because it satisfied one of their elective requirements for graduation.

By fifteen minutes into the class session, many of the students were numb, and a few were nodding off. Hadsell seemed to enjoy boring the class as it helped him focus on those that might rise to the occasion to challenge him. The others he didn't care about and often used a little sarcasm while looking for those who indicated they understood him with a smile. He paused between major points of the day's topic to take a drag on his little English cigar, flicking the ashes on the floor. Right away, he was talking about matters of history that were never discussed in traditional history or civics classes.

"Carefully scrutinizing The Communist Manifesto may help you understand the appeal of communism for many people," he started out.

High school teachers never talked about the Communist Party, Socialist Party, or others that existed in the 1950s. By doing so, they might have been suspected of being a member or affiliated with one of them. It's different for college professors. They talk about anything they want to. Graduate school professors say outlandish things. But challenging them at the graduate level was foolish as they could back it up with extensive analogies and facts, making the student with personal opinions look foolish.

"First," exclaimed Hadsell, "a communist's materialistic interpretation of history leaves no place for God. So, there is no need for absolute moral order and therefore no ethics or principles in government."

This was met with a few subdued hisses and boos from a few seemingly religious students in the class, but none dared take it any further for fear of being called out.

"Secondly, communism's political totalitarianism sees the individual as a subject of the state. The state only exists until a classless society evolves, then it is eliminated. And if man's so-called rights or liberties stand in the way of that end, they must be simply swept aside or eliminated. This includes his liberties of expression, his freedom to vote, his freedom to listen to what news and music he wants, and his freedom to choose what books to read."

"Take what I have just stated and apply it to religion. Churches desire to be totalitarian as well. They seek to keep the individual subject to the church and its leader's interpretation of the documents it has chosen to follow."

"The Catholics, for example, are taught to believe their church is the only true church. Therefore, the church is justified to use any means to convert whole civilizations to the dictates and control of the Catholic Church. History points out that's exactly what they have done and continue to do."

Several students got up and walked out.

"By the way, if any more of you find yourselves offended or uncomfortable understanding the role of religions in polarizing political views, I invite you to take some other class."

"Religions are guilty as much as governments in using force, violence, murder, and lying as a justifiable means to an end," he continued. "But the end can never be morally justified by a destructive means because, in the final analysis, the end is preexistent in the mean."

"Communism, with all of its false assumptions and evil methods, has grown as a protest against the hardships of the underprivileged. Communism, in theory, emphasizes a classless society and a concern for social justice. Though, in practice, the world knows from painful experience that it creates new classes and a new definition for injustice."

I found what he said interesting and challenged my existing knowledge as I sometimes didn't know what he was talking about. I knew my final grade would depend on understanding everything he discussed. I looked over at Benny, hoping to see him writing feverishly, and he was. I knew I would have to read his notes and the material more closely than I had been.

Chapter 21

MEANWHILE BACK AT THE RANCH

The volume of reading material was exhausting. There was just too much. Sometimes I had to reread passages two or three times to absorb them because the reading level required was more advanced than in high school. The slightest noise interrupted my concentration. After an hour of two, I was exhausted. Of course, during the rereading, I thought about having sex with Ginny.

There already wasn't much time left in the week to spend intimately with Ginny. The thought of fucking invaded my mind often, and I hoped that having sex several times a week would satisfy both of us. One night, my wrong perception of her sexual needs got corrected.

I tried to give Ginny my best that night. I was willing to accommodate her desires however she wanted, but she never asked for anything. It was hot and sweaty that night, even though the swamp cooler was loudly rumbling away. She seemed frigid, and I figured she was uncomfortable because everywhere our skin touched, it stuck together. She lay there motionless, expecting me to do her without any reciprocation. She only spoke out if I did something she didn't like. So, it was up to me to discover what she liked or didn't like, and I could only gauge that by whether she climaxed or complained.

I went down on her to break our skin contact as much as possible. I took my time, stopping at sensitive places to arouse her. She lay there motionless as if she didn't care one way or another. I slowly stimulated her with my tongue. I don't know how stimulating it was for her, but it was exceptionally arousing for me. After she became very wet, I worked my way upward to the clitoris, careful not to attack it like a vacuum cleaner.

I gently sucked on it, gradually increasing the flickering of my tongue and messaging her vagina with my index finger. She seemed to like what I was doing, but only for a little while, then she gently pulled on my hair to let me know she had had enough. I then rolled her over and tried entering her doggy style.

I was ready to explode. The site of Ginny was enthralling. Her totally nude body, the curve of her long torso leading to her shoulders and neck, and her long brown hair draping around her all enticed me with anticipation of ecstasy. I was on fire to cum. I wanted to penetrate her slowly, but she was so wet I started fiercely pumping away. She reacted with displeasure to my hips and testicles thumping against her thighs.

"I don't like it this way," she grumbled. I was so far gone I continued thrusting. I always wanted her to let me take her to climax, but she never would.

"Come on, Gin. Oh… God… "

She managed to move forward away from me as I was within moments of ejaculating.

"I'm not an animal," she said in an unsympathetic voice.

Confused, I remained on my knees, with a throbbing erection desperately needing release.

"I don't understand," I responded. "What is wrong with you?" I barked.

She hesitated to respond, then she came to her senses somewhat when she realized I hadn't climaxed.

"Just hurry up. I'm not in the mood, OK?" She rolled on her back and looked up at the ceiling, not making eye contact.

I was so far gone with a desire to ejaculate that I wasn't concerned with her mood. I stood at the edge of the bed and pulled her butt toward me. She gave up and gave in, and within moments I released in pleasure.

I helped her roll on her side to keep her from falling off the bed. She got comfortable in her usual sleeping position. At the same time, I stood there under the swamp cooler, sweating profusely, trying to cool down.

"God, it's hot in here," I said. "That swamp cooler isn't doing any good."

Ginny didn't move or say anything. I shut off the cooler, opened the window behind the bed headboard as wide as possible, and got back into bed. We lay there in the stillness of the night. I knew she wasn't asleep, but we had nothing to say to each other.

Suddenly, I heard the familiar grinding noise coming through the open window.

"There goes that sound again," I mumbled as I raised up and put my ear against the window screen. The sound was much louder than when it was coming through the wall.

"It sounds like it's next door."

I imagined it to be the leg of a piece of furniture rubbing against the floor.

"What the hell is he doing?"

The rhythm picked up its pace, and I could hear some distinguishable words within moments.

"Oh, Frankie. Oh. Oh, Frankie. Oooohhhh."

The rhythm suddenly stopped. All was quiet for a few seconds.

Then there was the sound of a toilet flushing.

No mistaking the sounds. The couple next door was having sex. I could have cracked a smile if it weren't for my jealousy of their passion.

I laid back down, staring at the ceiling. Why couldn't I arouse Ginny like that? It took a lot of foreplay to get any type of response from her. Only once could I remember getting her to climax from foreplay. I looked at her face when she was caught up in the moment, and her eyes were closed. In my anxiety, I wondered if she was thinking of someone else?

Chapter 22
THE CLASS GETS SMALLER

My classes, as well as my home life, continued with the same old routines. The Political Science class was noticeably smaller than before. I found Dr. Hadsell's lectures interesting, but others were bored and just trying to stay awake. I admit to getting drowsy occasionally. I knew I could count on Benny's notes to remind me of things I needed to review before the final if I missed anything during class. He faithfully kept taking notes every class. From the details of what he passed to the rest of us, he documented almost every word Hadsell said rather than just outlining the main ideas. Occasionally I could hear him rustling through pages of notes from earlier classes, perhaps to check for inconsistencies.

The Santa Ana winds were blowing dust-like sand through the classroom windows, but we were all too hot to do without any breeze passing through. Local students joked about the Santa Ana winds as Arizona topsoil blowing by in the Spring and back again in the Fall.

Hadsell never stopped talking.

"Marx viewed capitalism as essentially an irreconcilable struggle between the owners and the workers. The rich get exponentially richer while the poor get poorer. This was a far too simplistic view, but he made us aware of the gulf between superfluous wealth and object poverty. Aware of a real need for a better distribution of wealth, Marx revealed the danger of the profit motive as the sole basis of an economic system; capitalism is always in danger of inspiring men to be more concerned about making a living than making a life."

At that moment, I had a flashback of watching the pacifists from a top the Electric Boat parking structure with Taylor saying similar words to me - "We are prone to judge success by our salaries or the size of our automobiles rather than by the quality of our service and relationship to humanity."

My flashback was interrupted by a tap on my arm from Tommy passing me a note from Benny, which read, "SDS meeting tonight."

Hadsell continued talking, "In short, Marx convinces us that truth is not found in Marxism nor in traditional capitalism. Each represents only a partial truth."

His final remarks for the day were, "Capitalism fails to see the truth in a collective enterprise, and Marxism fails to see the truth in individual enterprise. Capitalism fails to see that life is social, and Marxism fails to see that life is individual and personal."

We were all anxious to vacate the roasting room except for Benny. He stayed behind to finish writing down the professor's concluding remarks verbatim.

Chapter 23
THE SDS MEETING

Ginny finished the dishes, walked into the living room, and turned on the TV. I turned to my reading as usual, as it was necessary to keep up. After only a moment or two, she turned off the TV and headed up the stairs toward the bedroom, apparently feeling ignored.

About an hour later, I met Tommy by my VW and drove us to the rally. It was a heated rally, like a union meeting before a strike.

"IBM is behind all this," bellowed out a student. "They're threatening to pull the defense research funding from the university unless they can continue influencing our curriculum to suit their agenda. I say good riddance IBM."

The crowd cheered in support.

"The administration is afraid of free speech because it might cause controversy," shouted another student. "They know that our organization brings people out of isolation and into the community, so they want all public gatherings stopped. They want us to be apathetic."

"I say we continue to organize for social change, especially if it affects their goddamned warmongering corporate profits," a third student chimed in. "Free Speech is the only way to break the establishment and the apathy of our fellow students."

The crowd cheered.

"We need to get IBM, Dow Chemical, and the rest of these evil bastards off the campus," another student yelled. "And they can take the ROTC with them. We need to be heard. We need those tables up."

The crowd cheered and started chanting, "Free speech. Free speech. Free speech."

Chapter 24

ROUTINES CHANGE, LINES DRAWN, TEMPERS FLARE

The next day Professor Hadsell stormed into the classroom. His demeanor made him seem angry and on the verge of outrage, and that was not like his usual reserved self. The students carried on isolated conversations.

"Alright, class, simmer down."

We all quieted down, noticing his unusual mood.

"Pass me the attendance sheet," he said gruffly.

He didn't seem to notice there were even fewer students than the week before. The attendance sheet, a yellow tablet, was located somewhere in the back of the room and passed forward. He took the tablet, ripped off the top sheet, crumpled it into a ball, and stuffed it into his coat pocket. This was confusing enough, but while doing it, he contradicted his action with his words.

"If you haven't signed it, please make sure you do to get credit for being here."

He knew he had confused us but motioned with his hands for us to stay seated and remain silent. This was a total change from his regular routine and alerted us that something was awry.

"Records are very important to the administration," he continued but was shortly interrupted by a student who began to ask a question.

"Prof, are we ..." Hadsell motioned for him to be silent.

Another student raised his hand.

"Yes, you have a question?" asked Hadsell while gesturing for him to remain silent as well.

The student caught on. "Eh…No sir, no question," replied the student.

"Good," replied Hadsell.

In silence, we watched the professor stand on his chair and then his desk. Then reaching above the exposed fire-sprinkler system pipe and gently feeling around for something, he pulled down a miniature microphone on a wire that had been taped to the pipe.

Students exchanged glances. I looked at my study group friends, who all looked back except Benny. Strangely he did not look up from his desk at first. Then he glanced at the professor, sheepishly watching Hadsell gently putting the microphone back into its hiding place. Then getting down from the desk, he waved for all ofus to get up and follow him out through the classroom door.

We assembled under the shade of a huge cottonwood tree. It was hot but bearable.

"This is as good a place as any to hold class," Hadsell began. "According to the department head, I'm being bugged. So from now on, at his suggestion, we will hold lectures away from the classroom because they might be misconstrued as subversive. I cannot express how irate I am."

"Why are they doing this?" asked Tommy. "We're not criminals."

"Criminal is a relative term depending upon one's point of view," retorted Benny.

Hadsell nodded affirmatively as he lit up another little English cigar. "You don't know whom you can trust these days."

"This is a University, for God's sake," said Tommy.

"Whoever and whatever they're after, I'm obviously under suspicion," responded Hadsell.

"You haven't done or said anything that's not within your right to say," I added.

"We ought to rip the Goddam wires out, the bastards," another student suggested.

"No. No violence," reprimanded Hadsell. "Violence isn't the cure for anything, and it'll just get me fired. If I'm gonna be fired, it's got to be over something bigger than having my classroom bugged."

"We don't have to take this," I said. "This is a free country. Wait till the SDS hears about this. They'll have a field day."

"All due respect to the Port Huron Statement, of which a lot of it is right in my opinion, this is not really my fight," said the Professor.

"But it can be ours," I added. By the mumbling, most students apparently indicated they agreed with me.

Benny took delight in putting Hadsell on the spot. "What do you suggest we do, Professor? Tell us."

Hadsell had a distorted look on his face. He struggled with what he could and probably should not say.

Finally, "Any success is made up of knowledge, persistence, and a lot of luck. All I can do is teach you what

I know. Perhaps that's enough knowledge, and the rest is up to you."

After more struggling with what to say, he solemnly started speaking again.

"Let me, for the record, tell you my opinion of the causes of all the events that are happening on this campus and on many other campuses. They are rooted in the ongoing struggle between the partial truths of communism and capitalism. Perhaps with a synthesis which reconciles both truths, we will someday arrive at an ultimate political system."

"Come on, Professor, can't you get to the point," I blew up. "What do we do in the meantime? What do we do now? What do we do today? Can't you..."

"The point, Mr. Sipe?" The Professor was caught in the crossfire of his assessment of things and what the college wanted him to say about the current events.

"Yes, the point," I repeated. We all knew that Hadsell was struggling with what to say.

"What do we do, Professor Hadsell?" It was an intense moment of truth for the Professor. He continued, somewhat remorsefully.

"What do we do today, tomorrow, and after that while we wait for the ultimate political system to prevail?"

Benny saw this as an opportunity to rub salt in Hadsell's wounds. "I-I-I believe that is the question, sir."

"Live life," the Professor suddenly blurted out.

Some students expressed displeasure with his answer. Even Benny stopped writing and laid his pen down.

"No, no. Hear me out," Hadsell spoke sharply. "Simply put, students, you must live life, and not just get through it, live it."

He looked at the floor as his demeanor changed from authority to regret, perhaps because of how he lived his life.

"Live life for yourselves, not for the state. Ask not what you can do for the nation. Ask what the nation can do for you. Let's get that right, at least."

What he said resonated with my conscience.

"You were not made for this nation. This nation was made for you. To give in to regulation is to degrade yourself to a status of a thing rather than elevate yourself to the status of a person."

I looked over at Benny. Of course, he was writing these words down.

Tommy wanted Hadsell to get to the point.

"So, what do we do today? And tomorrow? And the next? What do we do about Vietnam?"

Another student asked, "What do we do about IBM and ROTC?"

I joined in, "What do we do about restoring free speech on the campus?"

These types of questions were probably going to continue. Still, another student broke new ground,

"What can we do to promote free love?"

Many laughed, others chuckled, and even the Professor laughed as the mood was lightened.

"A collective voice can change the world," said Hadsell trying to pull the class back on track. "There's power and influence in numbers. But collective movements have to start with you individually. You must first take a stand. Take a stand on Vietnam. Take a stand on IBM and ROTC. Take a stand on free love if that means something to you."

More chuckling. Hadsell continued, "Second, never surrender. Submitting yourself to the state, the draft, or ROTC, makes you no better off than the people under Marxist rule."

"How can we not submit to the draft?" asked Tommy.

"Go for conscientious objector status," interjected Benny. "The law provides..."

"Easy to say but not easy to get," said Tommy. "Then go to Canada," said Benny in rebuttal. "What's that buy me?" questioned Tommy.

"Freedom!" said Hadsell retaking charge.

"Like in "Man Without A Country?" I asked.

"That's merely one perspective. If you are looking at Canada from ajail cell for the next five years, you might see things differently," Hadsell returned.

"You could take two years of alternative civilian service," barked another student.

"That would be compromise," said Hadsell. "Never compromise! The final rule. Never allow yourself to be used as a means to an end. The end does not justify the means and might does not make right. Alternative duty is duty nonetheless, and in prison, your liberties of expression are just muffled."

Hadsell lit another of his little cigars.

"If what I have said means anything, we must next take a closer look at the theory and potential of passive resistance. We must look to Gandhi."

A big crowd had gathered at the free speech area. However, not many groups and their tables had returned. Some of the groups were apathetic about the new rules. But the SDS made sure to be in full view of the administration building. The Assistant Dean came out shortly and zeroed in on Benny at the SDS table.

"You were instructed to take these tables down," he shouted at Benny. "I thought I had made that perfectly clear to you."

"I'm so-sorry," he countered, "my organization has not authorized me to take the table down."

"I am citing you for disciplinary action. Go into the administration building and meet with the Dean." Benny got up, and immediately another SDS member sat down in his place. The Assistant Dean tried to ignore the switch and proceeded to the next table.

"What don't you understand? Get this table down."

This was the 4-H club! They seemed much bolder than they had been the day before.

"I'm sorry, my organization has not authorized me to take the table down."

At that moment, any misguided ideas I had about farmers disappeared. I was proud of them for standing up for a cause that really wasn't their fight.

"Then I am citing you for disciplinary action as well," exclaimed the Assistant Dean. "Go meet with the Dean immediately."

The 4-H member got up, and immediately another member sat down in his place. The Dean was irate and unable to ignore the apparent revolt. He moved to the next table that dared to remain thus far.

"I am citing you too, if you don't move immediately," he said. Although the student from the Catholic Studies table wanted to stay, he gave in to the pressure and got up. None of the others in his group sat down in his place, and they began removing their literature from the table and packing up to leave.

"That's more like it," declared the Assistant Dean triumphantly. He turned back to the second table in victory. "I am citing you."

He pointed to the SDS table, "And you. Both of you go to the Dean's office now."

They looked at each other and to others in their respective groups for support. In a surprise move, an SDS member went over to the Catholic Studies table and stopped the members from breaking down the table by sitting down!

It was clear to the Dean that someone would always take the place of the person vacating a seat, so he stopped, glanced around, then stomped off toward the administration building.

The next day, the class was held under the tree as usual.

"The commotion with the Dean went all day," I said. Many in Hadsell's class chuckled.

Still referring to the previous day, I continued, "After almost all classes were over, they tried to start negotiating with the SDS table, but we told them that any agreement that fundamentally limited our doing what we've done in the past would not be acceptable."

"So, in effect," said Hadsell, "you limited the options in order to settle for what used to be".

"We will continue to escalate this tactic starting Monday," said Tommy.

"Speaking of escalation," said Hadsell, "I've been informed that the number of FBI agents and campus police have grown considerably, probably due to your activities and student unrest in general."

Some students made pig sounds. I glanced over at Benny and noticed that he sat silently with a face flushed.

"Class attendance has dropped across the campus as it has in our class, as you can see," continued Hadsell. "So, if campus classes are canceled for any reason, we can continue to meet at my home so you can still earn your credits."

It was common for graduate student classes to meet at public places or even private homes. This practice made graduate school so different from undergraduate school.

Chapter 25

MY RELATIONSHIP WITH GINNY EXPLODES

Friday night parties were another common occurrence on campus. Considering that most students had little money to spend, alcohol and pot were two affordable pleasures. Students could travel in groups to El Paso. To keep our cars from being stolen, we walked over the border bridge to Juarez to buy a quart bottle of Tequila for $3.00 and change. On campus, a lid or about an ounce of pot cost was $4.00. It was crude stuff and had to be cleaned of seeds and stems so it could be rolled into joints.

I recall one party at Tommy and Susan's house next door. The usual gang was all there. Jim and Glenda, Frankie and Mary, Tommy and Susie, and Benny and Judy. There were lively discussions on any topic. We boys were sitting around the coffee table where the Tequila with a bowl of sliced lemons and shot glasses were. We wanted to get buzzed quickly, and the conversations got personal as we did.

"Of course, we don't celebrate Christmas in my church," asserted Mary.

"Why is that?" questioned Tommy innocently.

"Because Christ didn't," responded Mary.

"He wasn't married either," said Benny as a matter of fact. Some laughed.

"Well, he never did have mu-mu-much to do with women," he added.

"Do you mean Christ was a queer?" snapped Mary. Laughter was louder because of her stupidity.

"Noooo," countered Benny. "I mean just that since he wasn't married, perhaps we shouldn't be?"

The group prepared to down another round of shots. I raised my shot glass, and the others followed suit.

"To friendship," I toasted.

"To friendship."

Jim had been hitting the Tequila steadily and was tipsy. He took another bite of his lemon slice, hoping it would help.

"Perfectly free! Perfectly single!" he blurted out.

"Well, guess who's not getting any tonight?" countered Glenda.

Ginny sat alone in a chair in the far corner of the room. I poured Jim and myself another shot. I was getting wasted too. We took lemon slices and followed the procedure.

"I've been wondering about marriage lately," said Ginny. "Why should we even get married? I mean, what's the point, especially if you're not going to have kids?"

"Guess who else is shut off!" I said to change the subject. Some of the group laughed.

"You mean I'm not already?" Ginny said, alluding to our almost non-existent sex life.

"The way you boys have been sticking together, I was beginning to think you were all queer," said Susie.

"Frankie sure isn't queer," said Mary.

"We know that," I emphatically stated.

I could not refrain myself. By this time, everyone knew I could hear them having sex through the shared wall at night, so I grabbed the coffee table leg and scraped it rhythmically against the floor, imitating what I heard through the wall.

"Oh, Frankie! Oh, Frankie! Oh, Frankie! Oooohhh, Frankieeeee!"

"What is he talking about, Frankie?" asked Mary, confused.

Frankie tried his best to ignore her question as we all chuckled.

Benny changed the momentum of the conversation.

"I propose we call a truce and take the women dancing. Whataya say, guys?"

"I'll drink to that," said Jim, who was already quite inebriated. I was too.

"I'll drink to anything right now."

Sergeant Benny pulled us all back into focus. "Three fast rounds, and we're on our way."

We filled up the shot glasses and reached for the lemon slices.

I don't know how we safely made it to the nightclub, but we did. As the gang exited the car, the girls took the lead toward the entrance door.

"Hey guys," said Frankie hanging back. "Hold up a minute." We held back. The girls waited at the door.

"It's OK. Go on in," shouted Benny to them. "We'll be there in just a minute."

"What's up, Frankie?" asked Tommy.

I felt guilty for imitating Frankie having sex, and I thought he might be going to address that situation.

"I hope it isn't what I said."

"Naw, it isn't that," said Frankie. "It's just that I'm quitting after this semester."

"Why? Your grades are OK," said Benny. "What's the problem?"

"Well, with the anti-war sentiment on campus and everything, we've decided to go back home to Boston. Mary's just not happy here. She's scared."

"Glenda's getting a little worried, too," said Jim. "We're thinking we're gonna lay low and not participate in anything for a little while if it gets any worse. I got a kid to worry about."

"Jesus, you guys," interjected Benny. "You're starting to scare me, and I'm starting to feel a little lonely here."

He looked over at Tommy. "I know Tommy's not going anywhere, at least."

Then he looked at me. "I suppose you'll be going back to submarines?"

I did a double-take. "I never told you about submarines."

He knew I hadn't and tried to cover his tracks. "Tommy told me, I guess. D-D-Didn't you, Tommy?"

"I may have. I don't remember," said Tommy.

"Anyhow, that's enough bad news for tonight," said Benny. "What do ya say we get fucked up and just have a good time tonight, eh?" He pulled out a joint.

"Damn. Far out," exclaimed Tommy.

"This is just the bud," said Benny. "It's the good shit, not the seeds and stems floating around the campus."

We passed it around several times, then entered Whiskey Dans' Night Club.

MAGIC CARPET RIDE – Steppenwolf

I like to dream, yes, yes
Right between the sound machine
On a cloud of sound I drift in the night
Any place it goes is right
Goes far, flies near
To the stars away from here
Well, you don't know what we can find
Why don't you come with me, little girl
On a magic carpet ride
Well, you don't know what we can see
Why don't you tell your dreams to me
Fantasy will set you free
Close your eyes, girl
Look inside, girl
Let the sound take you away
Last night I hold Aladdin's lamp
And so I wished that I could stay
Before the thing could answer me
Well, someone came and took the lamp away
I looked around, a lousy candle's all I found
Well, you don't know what we can find

Why don't you come with me, little girl
On a magic carpet ride
Well, you don't know what we can see
Why don't you tell your dreams to me
Fantasy will set you free
Close your eyes, girl
Look inside, girl
Let the sound take you away

...

Whiskey Dans' was inconspicuous on the outside. Storefront windows were covered, and only one small neon sign was over the entrance door. The parking lot was full as campus students already knew of the nightclub's existence. The inside was intentionally dark to give patrons the illusion of being incognito and private. The band was silhouetted- almost invisible and wound up the crowd with the whining guitar to the beginning of Steppenwolf's Magic Carpet Ride when we walked in.

Psychedelic Rock and Roll was the predecessor of Disco Music. It was inspired by the ever-increasing popularity of mind-expanding drugs like marijuana, LSD, and acid. Drug-induced mind states were enhanced by rock groups and the use of loud volumes from electronic instruments. The moving, pulsating, and constantly changing colors and patterns of psychedelic lighting, including strobe lights, disoriented the dancer and made them feel out of control. Which we were.

The girls wanted to dance even before we ordered drinks, so we went onto the raised dance floor. As the lyrics to the song started, strobe lights dominated a cascade of blinding multi-colored lights. It was psychedelic rock at its best. All was good. We started dancing as a group, then drifted apart, gradually changing partners as the music played.

Ginny danced with a stranger and kept dancing even after I had enough and left the dance floor. I sat there watching Ginny. She was dancing too close to this cowboy type. Much to my shock, he made sexual advances to her with his roving hands and made it obvious he wouldn't take no for his bid for sex. She was hot for attention, and he was giving it all he had. I thought I should intervene and made it to the edge of the raised stage when I realized they were exchanging words I couldn't make out over the music. I was stunned and felt stabbed in the heart when I saw the cowboy slip her a piece of paper, and she tucked it in her halter top rather than refuse it. With embarrassment, I returned to our table, planning to confront her when we got home. There I sat, hurt and confused about what I had seen

When the dance ended, the band took a break. While the rest of the gang returned to our table, Ginny returned a little later with the cowboy.

"Okay, to sit here?" he asked us.

Before anyone answered, "Yeah, sure," said Ginny.

No one else agreed with Ginny inviting this guy to sit with us, but no dissenting comment was heard. The girls seemed to surmise what was happening. They remained awkwardly quiet.

"My name's Buck."

His name drew a chuckle from Benny and the others.

"Okay, Buck. That name is suitable for you," said Benny sarcastically.

"What's the Wallace button for?" Benny questioned after noticing the election button pinned to Buck's jacket. "He la-lost, didn't he?"

"Rednecks love losers," said Tommy. "Bin losers since the Civil War, and they've gotten used to it."

"It don't matter," retorted Buck. "What is important is being a fighter, standing up, defending your rights, showing how tough you are. Wallace was the right man for the job."

Benny wasn't afraid of quoting the Wallace campaign. "Vote for law and order and for a God-fearing America."

"He gave a voice of hope in America," countered Buck.

I chimed in, "Wallace wanted whites to fear the negroes, so that gave rise to the phrase 'Fear in America.'

"You got that right," responded Benny. "Segregation now, segregation tomorrow, and segregation forever."

"The Negro has got out of hand," exclaimed Buck.

"What did the Negroes ever do to you?" I responded.

Buck was flustered. "It is a sad day in our country when you cannot walk in your neighborhoods at night because…."

"Because you're frightened of people that have dark skin?" I questioned. "I guess that makes sense," I said with contempt.

"It does," countered Buck. "Wallace talked common sense in easy-to-understand language and didn't make a complicated situation out of everything."

"He made it real easy to understand that he was a racist," said Benny.

"And a bigot," added Jim.

"And a cold-hearted political opportunist ... " then, imitating Wallace, I added, " ... I'll tell you what." Everyone began to mimic Wallace. Benny, "And I'll tell you what." Frankie, "And I'll tell you what." Tommy, "And I'll tell you what."

In his defense, Buck said, "You guys are listening to those wacko professors at the college. They want the commies to win. They say that's free speech, but they mean free speech only if you let them speak. They don't want anybody else to speak. And I'll tell you what."

We all laughed.

"Laugh if you want to," snapped Buck. "Wallace was for winning this war or getting out, and that's exactly what we should do. One or the other. And people understand that."

"Well then, I vote we get out," snapped Benny.

"Me too," said Tommy.

"Yeah, let's just get out," said Jim.

"The sooner, the better," added Frankie.

"They sure don't teach you boys anything about politics at that college," said Buck shaking his head back and forth.

We all looked around at each other.

"...and evidently, I'll tell you what, they don't teach you anything about good manners," retorted Buck.

"Like standing up for rednecks?" responded Benny.

I had had enough of the bantering about George Wallace standing up for America. Infuriated, I stood up.

"Yes, let's stand up for the rednecks," I said loudly.

We all stood up for the rednecks, and Buck headed for the door! "Just remember you're white, eh?" responded Buck. "Remember you're white!"

"What can I say?" asked Benny. "Th-that was in easy-to-understand Wallace lingo."

"How can we refute that? It wasn't complicated or anything," said Frankie.

"I guess we can't," added Jim.

"Guess he told us what," said Benny.

Tommy whipped out another joint and held it up so Buck could see it from the exit door. This was our way of flipping Buck off. Tommy finished his drunken thoughts by slurring, "To the horse, you rode in on. That's what," Then he lit the joint.

We all laughed.

I don't remember much more of that night. I don't remember Ginny and me getting home, but I do remember entering our front door, and the phone ringing. To the best of my recollection, this was the first time it rang since it was installed. I was unsteady and stumbled to answer it.

Upon answering the phone, the voice on the other end that I didn't recognize said, "Ginny, Ginny Sipe, please."

I turned to Ginny and extended her the phone, "It's for you." Woozy and feeling like I was about to black out, I sat on the stairs behind her and listened to her conversation.

She turned away from me and tried to muffle her conversation.

"Yes…yes, no, I don't think so…not a good idea," she whispered into the phone.

I struggled to remain in control, but the effects of the drugs were bouncing me from high to low and back again. I caught a glimpse of myself in the wall mirror and gazed at my reflection. It seemed I was outside of myself watching this other person.

Ginny continued talking to the caller. "No. I can't. Yes, I know where it is."

I tried to fight off the drugs.

"Who is it, Gin?"

She covered the telephone, figuring I was too far gone to understand her words. But I was instinctively alarmed by what she said and knew it was wrong. I tried to get up, but the drugs weren't about to let go of me.

"We got no secrets, Gin," I said, but I immediately fell back on the steps.

"I hear you," I heard her say. "Well…maybe, I don't know." Now, I wanted to know who was calling.

"No secrets," I mumbled.

I managed to pull myself back to reality enough to lunge for the phone. In reaction, Ginny turned away from me so quickly that my arm struck her in the face. She cried out and fell to the stairs. The phone fell to the floor, and I fell, trying to catch the phone. The drugs took effect again. I lay there on the floor next to the phone, unable to pick it up or get up, but I heard the caller's voice.

"Ginny, are you there? Ginny? I'll be waiting. Okay?" I returned to earth.

"Who was it? WHO WAS IT?" I demanded to know, expecting Ginny to start explaining.

She was in pain. I was stupefied.

The telephone was beeping loudly to remind me that it was off the hook. Sobbing, Ginny began to climb the stairs toward the bedroom. I tried unsuccessfully to hang up the phone but just gave up and started up the stairs. There was one light at the head of the stairs. Finally overtaken by the drugs or letting myself be overtaken, I struggled to reach the light. It became my goal. The light began to get brighter and brighter, and then I don't remember anything after that.

Sometime in the middle of the night, I suddenly awakened and sat straight up from my stupor, sweating profusely. Once I realized where I was, I looked toward Ginny. Ginny was not in bed. I stumbled out of bed, hurriedly put on my blue jeans and t-shirt, and staggered through every room in the house. Ginny was nowhere to be found. I even went to see ifour car was there. She was gone. Instinctively, I knew with whom she was with. I was consumed with anger, resentment, and rejection. Confused and helpless, I ran wildly across the parking lot and out of the village into the dark desert. I stopped a short ways out when I realized what dangerous creatures lurk among the scrub and sand dunes at night. All was silent except for the crickets. I looked up into the stars and let out an exceedingly long and loud primeval scream.

"Nnnnoooooooooooooo!"

Tommy was the only one I could think of that might help me get my shit together. I knocked loudly on his door, and Tommy finally answered, opening the door cautiously at first.

"Hey, Weldon, man. What's wrong?"

"I need your car. Let me borrow your car," I said, trying not to scramble my words.

"Sure, man. Okay. What's wrong? Where's your car?" he replied.

"She's with him," I stammered. "I know she is. I'm going to find her before it's too late."

Tommy also guessed who she was with and that it was probably too late.

"That bastard! I'll get the keys."

FREEDOM (LIVE) - Richie Havens: The bongo's intro followed by:

Freedom, freedom …

Sometimes I feel
Like a motherless child

Sometimes I feel
Like a motherless child

Sometimes I feel
Like a motherless child

A long Way From my home
…

I drove Tommy's car. Assuming they were in a motel somewhere, I roamed up and down the strip on the edge of town. Slowing down as I passed The Nights Peace Motel; I had a feeling about the place. It looked like a seedy place for one-night stands. It had cars parked with their license plates facing the motel rather than toward the street where they could be readily identified. This one was definitely a no-tell motel. I did a quick U-turn and entered the motel parking lot. Sure enough, there was my red VW!

My knees quivered as I slammed the car door and approached the office. The door was lit by a flickering yellow neon light that accented the door-handle hole in the screen door where people before me had to pry it open as there was no handle. There was a sign on the door saying, "No soliciting."

I approached the desk. The clerk was a motherly type of woman wearing an apron. She had been doing the dishes in the kitchen that was visible behind her.

"Yes?" she said sternly.

I wanted to be anywhere but there, but I had to find Ginny. I sputtered my words and pointed outside through the picture window in the office.

"That's my car," I said, feeling choked up. "My car there in that parking space. Right there."

"Whose car?" she sternly replied.

"Mine," I said. "I mean mine and my wife's. She's here with him. I can't remember his name!"

I was not sure if she understood me or if she was playing dumb. "Did you want a room for the night?"

"No, I don't want a room! I just want to know where she is. Where is she? Where?"

Having no empathy or understanding for my situation, she said, "Wait a minute, Sonny. Who? Who's she?"

With total frustration, I emphatically said, "My wife! Ginny. Ginny Sipe."

The woman began looking through the registration cards. "Ginny, Ginny Sipe,"

She mumbled as she rifled through them, then suddenly gave up, "I'm sorry, but no Mrs. Sipe is registered here."

"Of course not!" I reacted. "She's here with him! She wouldn't sign! Where are they?" I was frustrated and looked through the front window at the cars in the parking lot, trying desperately to find a clue as to where she might be.

"I can't tell from where the car is parked."

Quickly the woman went to the door that led to the living quarters. Her husband was drying the dishes while watching television. "Fred? Better come in here."

Fred entered with a dish towel over his shoulder. "Yes, Mama. What's wrong?"

"Boy says his wife's here with another man."

Fred approached me as the woman continued, "Tell him, Fred. Tell him what you always say."

He leaned uncomfortably close to my face.

"Yes, Son. Well, look at it this way. The competition's pretty rough in this motel business, I tell you. I don't get nosey about your business, and you don't get nosey about mine. And we run a Christian place here; don't take no transients we don't think are God-fearing folk. Now, if you wish to upset the God-fearing people here, I could call the Police for you. That is if you want to make a disturbance, disturb the peace. Now, Son, I'd jest suggest...."

In total desperation, I started to lunge for his tie. I managed to stop my action, jerk open the screen door and exit into the parking area.

FREEDOM (LIVE) - Richie Havens: continues with the second verse:

Sometimes I feel
Like I'm almost gone

Sometimes I feel
Like I'm almost gone

Sometimes I feel
Like I'm almost gone

Yeah, a long, long...
Long way from my home
...

My pride was crushed. My fidelity to our marriage was meaningless. I was utterly confused, disoriented, and totally hysterical. My anger took over, and I ran along the lower row of motel rooms, screaming and pounding on each door.

"Come out, you whore! Come out, you bitch!" My yelling got louder as I progressed. "You slut! Whore! Fucking bitch! I know you're fucking in there!"

I am sure Ginny was able to hear me outside. A few others peered through their window curtains. One or two turned on their stoop lights, but no one seemingly dared open their door because my foul language indicated my high level of anger.

Then a door opened in the distance, and Ginny, half covered by a bedsheet, came rushing out with Buck tugging on her trying to get her back into the room.

"No, I said. Stop," Ginny yelled at Buck.

She struggled, finally pulling away from him.

"Show me, girl," Buck responded. "You can take it, can't you? You like it."

"You're a goddam pig," she yelled back.

"What do you think you're doing, bitch?" exclaimed Buck.

He yanked the sheet away, leaving Ginny naked, then backhanded her. She recoiled in pain.

"Go back to your hippy husband. Your nothing but a cold popsicle."

"You misguided asshole," she said as she picked up the sheet and haphazardly covered her naked body.

She hadn't noticed me yet.

"The only thing that works on you is your dick," she yelled.

When she saw me, she said, "Weldon, you're here?"

I held up my hand, signaling her to not come any closer.

"Was it worth our marriage? Was it? That's what it cost you. Maybe it was a mistake bringing you to New Mexico. All I had to offer you was my loyalty. I'm sorry if that was not enough."

I turned away from her, heading toward Tommy's car, disappearing into the shadows. I was devastated when I reached it, and I broke down sobbing.

Chapter 26
MY NEW LIFE BEGINS

On one hand, moving into the college dormitory was a life change. On the other hand, I realized that I was entering the dating scene again, which had good and bad things about it. The bad thing was that it wasn't my choice, but the good thing was that girls were plentiful.

The longer I was away from Ginny, the clearer it became to me that she was not happy with me, her life, or where she was going. Worst of all, I didn't know why. I was never to know why. But I did know that there was nothing I could do about it.

I pulled up to the college dormitory. Sitting on the second-level railing was a cowboy-looking character in a plaid shirt, blue jeans, cowboy hat, and boots, smoking a cigarette. When I checked in with the student housing administration, I was told I would have an agricultural student as a roommate, his name was Bud. I guess I was expecting a forest ranger type, not a cowpoke. All he needed to complete his attire was chaps, spurs on his pointed-toed boots, and an old pick-up truck with a shotgun rack hanging in the cab window.

My VW was stuffed completely. I grabbed what I could carry, including a floor lamp, my portable typewriter, and a load of clothes slung over my shoulder. I struggled with the floor lamp because it was made to swivel, which it did from side to side, banging against the rod iron railing of the stairs. Bud watched me struggling in silence, with a smirk on his face. He didn't offer to help.

When I caught up to him, he spoke, "You a hippie?"

I immediately realized that to him, I probably did look like a longhaired hippie.

"I'm about as much a hippie as you are a fence-mending cowpoke," I muttered as I continued passed him. I tried not to look at him directly but kept him in my peripheral vision, just like you would a bull in a pasture. If the bull decided to charge for any reason, you would see when to start running for the fence. Looking at him directly might make him mad, and he would charge.

I assumed the open dormitory door behind him was our room, so without making eye contact, I headed in. When I returned for another load, Bud was nowhere to be seen. I spent the rest of the day unpacking alone.

By dinner time, Bud finally showed up. I was typing at my desk by the light of my partially broken floor lamp. Bud sat on his bed and proceeded to roll a cigarette. The process was fascinating to watch.

I watched with occasional glances. Bud would take a piece of cigarette paper from a small packet in his shirt pocket and form a u-shaped trough using his finger. He poured some tobacco into it from a string-drawn pouch pulled from his other pocket. Then, licking the edge of the paper, he gently rolled it up with the tobacco to form a cigarette. His spit was sufficient to glue it together. Then, to finish his routine, he laid down with his cowboy hat still on, and his boots over the edge of the bottom of the bed frame. Finally, he reached over to his desk radio beside him and turned on some old-time country music.

I describe country music as harmonized depression. They are always lonely, and bitching about something.

The song he was listening to was no exception. After thirty seconds, I couldn't take any more of it and had to say something.

"Why are they always whining about something? My dog died, and I got fired. My woman left me, and the bank took my house."

Bud didn't respond. He just laid there with his lit hand-rolled cigarette tightly between his lips.

I figured the only way I would have peace again was to turn on my radio to some hard rock loud enough to drown out the cowboy's radio, so that's what I did.

Bud's eyes popped open, and speaking out the side of his mouth over his cigarette he said, "What the hell is that? Sounds like a heap a loud noise."

"It's rock and roll, man!"

I turned up the volume to drive my point home. Bud was perturbed but in a typically reserved cowboy kind of way. He bit down on his smoke, rolled his eyes, turned his head away.

Finally, he muttered, "Loud is good. It'll drown out the sound of my puking if I have to listen too much more."

He made his point. I didn't want to have a serious confrontation on the first night of our honeymoon, so I turned the volume of my music down. Bud reciprocated by turning his music off, and then I turned mine off.

Bud was reading one of his Agriculture textbooks while taking tiny puffs of his cigarette held pursed between his lips.

Soon he fell asleep, and his textbook slid off and onto the floor. His cigarette continued to burn, and I kept glancing over, expecting his bed cover to soon be on fire.

I turned back to my typewriter. My class choices indirectly influenced me to be active in taking control of my future, whatever it might be. So, on my first day in my new dorm life, I realized that my situation was temporary, and nothing was holding me back from making life changes.

I made a fundamental decision about the military draft – I was not going into the military. I accepted that there would be possible consequences, but I did not put too much thought into how serious they might be.

I made inquiries via letters exploring my options on opportunities for avoiding the draft. One was to The War Resisters League in Niagara to inquire about requirements for immigration to Canada. A second letter was sent to The Central Committee for Conscientious Objectors in Philadelphia for information and guidance on refusing to be drafted for military service.

Bud was snoring with the burning cigarette still in his mouth. I watched him between writing letters, amazed that he continued to let his cigarette burn until it had to be burning his lips. I figured his snoring might cause him to inhale the butt, but he suddenly awoke when he felt the burn. He threw his smoldering butt in the ashcan, sat up, and rolled another one. He lit it and resumed his restful pose, tightly holding his new cigarette between his lips. In a way, I admired this drugstore cowboy.

I turned back to my typewriter and wrote a final letter. It was to Local Board No. 167, Greensburg, PA.

"Dear Sirs: This letter is to inform you that in the event I am drafted, I will not, under any circumstances, enter the Armed Forces. I hereby desire to apply for Conscientious Objector Status 1-A-O because I cannot condone war in any form."

I sealed the letter and laid it aside. Glancing over to Bud, I saw that he was awake, and I was getting hungry. Ginny wasn't around to cook for me, and there was no pantry or refrigerator full of food.

"Say listen Hop-A-Long," I said to Bud, "I know we're not exactly friends, but since I'm apparently single again, where do we get something cheap to eat?"

"Well, that depends, hippy. How much of a man are you?" was his reply.

"What?" I said.

"How 'bout Mexican. Real Mexican."

"I never ate Mexican," I said. "What's in it?"

"You like spicy?" he questioned.

"You mean like Tobasco sauce?" I asked.

He smiled a little. "Kinda," was his reply.

Dicks Café was a house that had been converted into an authentic hole-in-the-wall Mexican restaurant. Inside was typical Mexican improvised décor. The walls were painted green and orange, with some felt paintings hanging randomly depicting desert cacti and men wearing sombreros. Everything was functional, but the tables were different sizes, and the tablecloths didn't match. Dick was the heavy-set, non- English-speaking owner. He served as the waiter and was the cook too. Bud spoke a little Spanish, as most all native south-westerners did.

The menu was in English, but the item descriptions were foreign.

Dick brought us a small bowl of what looked like peppers.

"These here is Jalapenos," said Bud. "Like an appetizer, in a manner of speaking. You just grab hold of the stem and eat the whole pepper like this."

He ate the pepper without flinching, so I figured it was all right.

"Good shit. Try one," Bud said as he ate another.

I took one, bit off the stem, and chewed it up. Shortly, I was in a full body spasm, unable to get rid of the increasing burn.

Almost hoarse from the burn, I garbled, "Holy Shit!"

I grabbed a glass of water and tried to gulp the heat away.

Bud was delighted at my predicament. "Burns twice as bad when it comes out your ass," he said with a grin.

He translated the Spanish ingredients for me to find something I might like. I was surprised to discover that most dishes had rice, beans, cheese, lettuce, tomato, and different hot peppers. My mouth was still burning when we left the Café.

"Feel like a beer?" Bud asked as we climbed into his beat-up red pickup truck.

"Considering I'm probably going to shit myself to death, yeah. Maybe two, or three, or four!" I responded.

His truck had battered upholstery and a missing door panel on the passenger side. It ran rough but seemed reliable. It smelled like straw, his rolled cigarettes, and I could imagine him using it to herd cattle and mend fences. I glanced through the rear window into the truck bed. Sure enough, there were a couple of fence posts, barbed wire, and a few empty beer cans rolling around.

The Hitching Post Cantina had cowboys, cigarette smoke, beer, and nude dancers. The music fit the scene. Most cowboys were alone and sad, mesmerized by the dancers and crying in their beers. One was sleeping in the corner with his boots up on the table. The bartender looked like he'd rather be someplace else.

SEEDS AND STEMS AGAIN - Commander Cody & His Lost Planet Airmen

Well, I'm sittin alone, Saturday night,
watching the Late Late Show.
A bottle of wine, some cigarettes,
I got no place to go.
Well, I saw your other man today;
he was wearing my brand-new shoes,
And I'm down to seeds and stems again, too.
Well, I saw my old friend Bob today

from up in Bowling Green;
He had the prettiest little gal
that I'd ever seen.
But I couldn't hide my tears at all,

cause she looked just like you,
And I'm down to seeds and stems again, too.
Now everybody tells me
there's other ways to get high.
They don't seem to understand
I'm too far gone to try.
Now these lonely memories,
they're all I can't lose,
And I'm down to seeds and stems again, too.
Well my dog died just yesterday
and left me all alone.
The finance company dropped by today
and repossessed my home.
But that's just a drop in the bucket
compared to losing you,
And I'm down to seeds and stems again, too.
Got the Down to Seeds an Stems again Blues.

...

We sat at the bar next to a small stage. I found the locals more interesting than the dancers. I don't get the allure of titty bars. Why pay for something you can't have?

The nude dancer on the stage, under the colored lights, tried to dance sexually to the slow, sad song, but it came off awkwardly. The cowboys loved her anyway and watched her intently. Any one of them would take her home if given a chance. Even Bud studied the dancer intently when she took her top off. I sipped my beer and looked around the bar.

Nearby was a group of 5 inebriated cowboys. One of them was talking to the others and pointing at me, and they must have noticed I was inattentive to the dancer. Shortly the group came over to our table and gathered around us.

"Don't like tits?" said the one that pointed at me.

I tried to ignore them, but they weren't going to leave. "You a queer?" another one asked.

I had had enough.

"Well, seems this place is mostly filled with lonesome cowboys gawking at a couple of tits while they're holding hands," I said. "So, if I'm queer, what does that make you?"

That was apparently the wrong thing to say. The next thing I knew, I was hustled into the parking lot under some large neon commercial beer signs in a clearing among the many pick-up trucks. The group of cowboys and some others gathered around me.

I was so surprised by this whole event that I didn't respond when the hitting began.

"Fight you, goddam queer. Fight!" said the cowboy, that initially pointed a finger at me.

"Kill the long-haired commie!" said another.

On the second blow to my stomach, I fell to the ground, windless. I caught a glimpse of Bud near the exit door. He couldn't stand that I made no attempt to fight back and suddenly jumped in the fight but was immediately pushed back against a truck by several cowboys. He took several blows to the stomach and dropped to the ground.

"Now, this ain't really your fight, partner," said one of them. "I suggest you pick better friends."

The cowboys made their point that I wasn't welcome there, but I think out of respect for Bud being one of their own, they backed off and went back inside.

I regained my breath and hobbled over to Bud, and we helped each other up. Still angry, Bud immediately started to go back into the bar, but I stopped him.

"Hey, don't you look at the odds before you get into a fight?"

He came to his senses with the realization that we were outnumbered. He finally managed a little laugh, "Well, that's enough fun for one night anyway." We both hobbled toward the truck.

The following day, Bud came in with the mail. I was awake and reading at my desk.

"Why wouldn't you fight?" he asked. "You don't strike me as a pansy."

"In case you didn't notice, we were outnumbered," I replied. "So, I resorted to protecting myself, I guess."

Bud said nothing more on the subject and sorted through the mail. He found something addressed to me and dropped it on my desk.

I picked it up. The letter was from The Selective Service System— Local Board No. 167. I nervously opened it.

"Greetings from the Office of the President," it said. "You are hereby ordered to report for Induction. "

I stopped reading it, folded it back up, put it back into the envelope, and laid it on my desk. I knew what it was, and I wasn't going to deal with it right then. I looked over at Bud, and he was rolling another cigarette.

"Mind if I try one of those?" I asked.

Bud tossed his sack of tobacco to me, followed by his little packet of cigarette paper and a zippo lighter.

"That bad, eh?"

"Let's say it's a perfect ending to a perfect week," was my reply.

Bud propped his feet up on the foot of the bed frame, took a puff, then watched me roll a perfect cigarette. I laid back just like he did, and took a puff.

"I am impressed," he said with his little smile.

Chapter 27
THE HORNETS NEST BECOMES DISTURBED

The number of FBI on campus increased to where it was noticeable to the students. Anti-war notices were everywhere, tacked or taped to poles and bulletin boards. As often as the FBI tore them down, new ones were put up.

Hadsell became paranoid, and he moved the class to his house. We sat around a large low coffee table, eating all kinds of free junk food and sodas that kept us from leaving.

The lighting was low and gave the room an uncanny resemblance to the famous rendering of the Last Supper. Most students seemed randomly engaged and were somewhat inquisitive while indulging in the free munchies.

"Love thy neighbor," Hadsell began the discussion for the day. "Turn the other cheek. These two Christian principles can bring about world peace in a world violently opposing peace."

"Gandhi discovered in using these principles to resist violence, he became violently non-violent in resisting evil."

Some students laughed a little at this wordplay but became fascinated despite themselves.

"But, Prof, I can love something or someone that I know is not at all good for me," said an engaged student.

"Yes, that,s right," said the professor. "We do call affection love. But in a deeper sense, love means much more than something that can be 'got off on., Love is redemption, a sequel to social justice and faith in the possibilities of all human beings."

"The silent majority doesn't give a fuck for my possibilities!" spoke another provoked student. "Their silence makes it obvious they're violently opposed to them!"

"It may take violence to overcome violence," said Hadsell. "You need violence to right the wrongs, but Ghandi discovered that violence could be passive resistance."

Sideline conversations between students stopped giving him their attention because they were trying to understand his logic.

I had a problem with that logic. "How can violence be passive? If I go against the establishment to be heard, it sure as hell has to be more authoritative than just passive."

"Well. Yes. Sure," agreed the Professor. "But you can actively resist the evil non-violently. You don't want to humiliate your opponent. You want to win his friendship and understanding. Passive resistance means you must persuade those doing wrong to see that they are wrong."

"What if he won't listen to what I'm trying to say?" I asked.

"Protest. Boycott. Fail to cooperate. Try to make him see that he is the victim of his failure to listen to you. And as long as he is unwilling to hear the truth, he allows himself to be victimized by the lie, and he has no possibility of redemption."

"Speaking of redemption," said Benny, "I have a confession to make."

This broke the tempo of the lesson, and it quickly became quiet. "Until a few days ago, I-I-I was working for the FBI."

Everyone was stunned.

"I was the one who bugged the classroom because they wanted more proof than my notes on things that the professor was saying."

The class was horrified. Benny looked directly at Hadsell. "For this, I am truly sorry, Professor. I thought I was being a patriot, but I started feeling more and more like a Judas."

Hadsell remained silent, trying to process the situation. Benny produced the tapes from his jacket pocket and laid them on the table.

"Here are the tapes. I told them that the recorder malfunctioned."

"Why did you do it?" asked the Professor.

"I don't know," said Benny glumly. "Maybe I got caught up in being part of their solidarity. The truth is, I've listened to those tapes at least a dozen times and looked at my notes repeatedly, and you are right. God help us all. Gandhi, Jesus Christ, and you are right. At the time, I thought I was right, that I was doing what had to be done. I'm sorry. Really, I am."

He got up to leave. "Where will you go?" I asked him.

"Home. I am going home, I guess, to start over again." Benny left.

We were all dumbstruck.

"Thus, the end is surely reconciliation," said Hadsell.

"Reconciliation?" I barked. "To what? How is there reconciliation in what just happened?"

"Benny left peacefully, didn't he?" said Hadsell.

"Yes, but I don't feel peaceful about it."

"Maybe not," said Hadsell. "But you can find happiness in his willingness to face the truth. He has saved himself from being the victim. He has freed himself to seek total redemption and reconciliation with you, his friends, and his immediate community."

There was grumbling among the students. They were bewildered because it seemed he was on a tangent that they could not follow or understand.

Hadsell continued to expound, "We must all learn to be reconciled to the notion that a beloved community can exist. Oh, we don't have it, not by a long shot! Or even anything like it. But isn't it something we hope to redeem? Isn't that what Universities are really for, to reflect the universe in your ideas? Isn't that why you're here?" He made it worse. "To see the real possibility of a beloved community, a country, an existence to love? Where we would love to be doing what we're doing and what others are doing. And our commonality would reside in this love. A beloved country for us all and for all our loves, all kinds of our loves!"

He saw that he had gone too far as he tried to save the virtue of the lesson. He was over the edge. We knew we would have a final exam, so we couldn't dismiss what was being said.

Since Benny left and was not taking notes, we realized we would not have anything to learn from and review.

"So, we are here, you say, only to study possibilities?" I asked. "I don't remember ever coming across a Possibilities Department, and can you get a Ph.D. in it?"

There was some general laughter at this challenge. Professor Hadsell was dismayed.

"Well, perhaps there should be such a department. It's painful to live only on expectations, sometimes violently painful."

I found myself wishing Benny was there to say something, but to my surprise, Jim rose to the occasion.

"So, you're saying we are here to just sit around and moan because we don't have a slice of a satisfactory pie. Is that it?"

The little bit of laughter died down as the sad truth emerged. "Yes. In a sense," replied Hadsell.

He took up a book and began reading, though he didn't have to keep his eyes always on the page; he knew it almost by heart.

"The nonviolent resister must be willing to accept violence, if necessary, but never to inflict it. If rivers of blood have to flow before we gain our freedom, it must be our blood. The nonviolent resister does not seek to avoid jail. If going to jail is necessary, he enters it as a bridegroom enters the bride's chamber," Hadsell read.

He looked up for a moment.

"For us, I think that means to build and live freely in a beloved country."

Then he went back to reading.

"We turn the other cheek because unearned suffering is redemptive. Suffering is infinitely more powerful than reasoning or the law of the jungle for converting the opponent and opening his ears which are otherwise shut to the voice of reason."

He closed the book. The students responded with a kind of mumbling dissatisfaction. Some started subdued rebuttal conversations.

"Sounds like pie-in-the-sky to me," refuted Tommy. Some others thought it seemed absurd.

"So just take it, huh? That's easy for you to say! But how much can we be expected to endure? And why?" continued Tommy.

"I know. I know. I wonder, too," said the Professor apologetically.

Some stood up, ready to leave, and a few did. Hadsell spoke faster to try to keep others from leaving.

"If you have faith in the future, you can justify the suffering by believing that the universe itself is on the side of justice and that there is a creative force, call it Love, that works for universal wholeness. There you will live in a whole new beloved country."

From the look on the professor's face, it was apparent that he knew he was asking too much of us and had left us only with unresolved anger and frustration.

In the next few moments of silence, the other students left. Tommy and I lingered, perhaps not wanting to displease Hadsell or perhaps hear more. It was an awkward situation, but we just couldn't be rude to the professor. Part of me wanted to understand the depth of what he had said.

I had been present for all his lectures, and this was his most philosophical one.

"Do you understand? I'm afraid they don't," he said. "I have probably done more harm than good. All I meant was that we can live without a country or recreate a better one."

Seeing that we didn't abandon him gave him the courage to go on but at a much lower volume.

"Gandhi believed that nonviolence could heal his country and that the healing process could recreate another country, a better one, one we can call beloved."

He was on a roll again. Tommy and I looked away, now a little embarrassed to leave. Professor Hadsell's eyes glazed over with a despairing look. Tommy broke the silence.

"Hey, Weldon, I have to go. Susan will wonder..."

"Yeah, sure," I interrupted. "I'll go with you."

As we headed for the door, Professor Hadsell called to me.

"Weldon? Why can't you believe that instead of living without a country, you might, perhaps, somehow, create a better one?"

"I'll give it some thought," I replied.

And I did. I couldn't sleep that night thinking about all Hadsell had said and what results I could expect from my letter to the Draft Board.

Chapter 28
PUSH COMES TO SHOVE

I awoke incensed to Hadsell's lecture from the previous day just as Bud came in from an early morning class.

"There is a large crowd gathered in the free speech area," he said. "How come you're not there?"

I dressed quickly and headed for the free speech area outside Hadley Hall. My frustration grew with every step. What would be the outcome of the protests and anti-war movement? What was the point of it all?

As I walked past the cafeteria heading for the free speech area, I passed the row of steel newspaper dispenser boxes. I did a doubletake when I saw the headline on one of them. I didn't have any change, so I bent down to read what I could see through the glass.

The headline read: "US LOSES SECOND NUCLEAR SUB - THE SSN579. The article went on say that the Stingray rests 10,000 feet down in the Atlantic. All 124 officers and 5 civilian technicians aboard were lost. General Dynamics Electric Boat, the builder of the submarine, and the Navy Bureau of Ships, were jointly conducting warfare tests. In their official report, the Navy's leading experts in submarine design advised the Navy Court of Inquiry that the US nuclear submarine Stingray sank because of a violent explosion of the main storage battery. The Navy depended upon this performance to the extent that it had asked for and had already received the authority to build 14 of these ships with the same characteristics. This was the first time since World War II that we were constructing a large class of general-purpose attack submarines."

It was a stab to my heart since I was chosen as one of five original technicians. It could have been me at the bottom of the Atlantic! It would have been me! I couldn't help but wonder who was the poor bastard that took my place. While going through training for the mission, I overheard some Navy personnel refer to the five of us as NUBs. As we were leaving New London, I asked a neighboring Navy submariner living in our apartment complex what a NUB was. He hesitated in telling me, but seeing that I was moving away, he explained, 'non-useful being.' Apparently, we were expendable passengers and there only to observe and report to General Dynamics what broke as we were sinking. That upset me but made sense considering all the quick study of systems and component drawings.

I hurriedly continued toward Hadley Hall. With every step, all previous events leading up to now became part of my growing anger. I had been bottling up anger from my Electric Boat days. Did the ship's doom have anything to do with what I overheard the two dock workers talking about on the scaffolding?

This was the tipping point toward my anti-war stance. I was determined to do what I could to stop all the sinister madness. Taylor was right. War has no winners, and the victor, if there is one, is not right because of winning. He's merely still standing.

Bud was right. A large crowd had gathered. Larger than ever. I walked forcefully through the crowd and headed straight for the SDS table. The table was now twelve feet long with a dozen people and a large banner saying, "Protect your right of free speech and the rights of your fellow students."

The Assistant Dean was at the table, too, with a couple of campus policemen. I stood beside Tommy.

"I want you to remove this table, and all of you leave this instant," blared the Assistant Dean through a bullhorn.

It looked as if they were going to disperse. I couldn't contain letting out my emotions. It was just going to be the same scenario over and over again. I suddenly jumped up on the table and began speaking. I hadn't planned on this, and I didn't know what I was going to say, so I started with the apparent purpose of having the table.

"Free speech is a right guaranteed by the constitution of the United States, a constitution of, by, and for the people. We live in a democratic system and will not be manipulated into agreeing that this right is only for the powerful and elite."

The Assistant Dean replied to this basic premise. "What do you people think you're accomplishing by all this?"

"We want retribution for the students suspended or thrown off campus." The words spewed from my mouth. "We want the restoration of free speech for all students. We have a right to exercise free speech on this campus."

There was some cheering as I gained more attention.

The Assistant Dean avoided debating the constitution. "Free speech is not the issue here. It's your insolence."

He took out a notepad from his jacket and opened it to a clean sheet.

"What is your name?"

My knees were shaking, but I stood my ground and remained silent. I was not going to back down.

The Assistant Dean realized that I was committed to the cause.

"In that case," he spoke with profound authority, "You're going to be arrested and removed from this campus."

He motioned to the Campus Security that he had called in to detain me until the Police arrived. Although Campus Security was there at his request, it was evident by their hesitance that they didn't really expect to detain anyone.

What happened next is still unclear, but as they moved in on me, I jumped over them and onto the stucco frame of the freedom bell. Then, climbing to the top, I straddled the headstock and shouted to the crowd.

"Our administration has outlawed the use of this free speech area because anything we think is important, anything we care about, and anything we want to talk about seems to be too controversial for IBM and Dow Chemical."

HADLEY
ADMINISTRATION

The crowd began quickly gathering around me at the foot of the bell. Some yelled, "right on," while others began whistling and applauding. The Campus Security wasn't committed enough to their orders to climb up after me. They stood at the base, looking as if they somewhat supported me.

I continued shouting whatever came to my mind.

"You hear the administration use the term 'outside agitator.' They are referring to their perception of hard-core protesters who travel from one campus to another, initiating and provoking trouble. Well, where are they? I don't see them. I am a student on this campus, just like you. And the only outside agitators I know about on this campus are IBM, Dow Chemical, and the ROTC."

The Assistant Dean motioned to Campus Security to move in. They tried to grab my feet but could not dislodge me from the bell, so they waited on the ground as a lion would wait for his prey to fall out of a tree.

"Our administration sacrifices our free speech for public relations with the real outside agitators. The silence of our professors is being bought. The grants and huge sums of money given to this University from the defense industry are dictating the content of our curriculum. Our research and skills are being developed for investors in the arms race."

Some students formed a barrier around the bell, pushing back the Campus Security and shouting, "Let him speak."

"The university has become a factory to produce people who will fit the specifications of their clients. They don't want square pegs that won't fit into round holes," I continued.

The Campus Policemen tried to half-heartedly break through the barrier but couldn't.

"President Eisenhower warned us about the Military Industrial Complex. Workers across America are enslaved into making weapons of mass destruction. War has become big business. These weapons are powerful enough to destroy not only our so-called enemies but ourselves at the same time. And still, the weapons industries manage to convince president after president that we need more. When is enough, enough?"

The newly arrived State Policemen drew their sticks. Maybe the pushback was too much, or the disrespect angered them, but they managed to break through this time. I tried kicking their hands away, but once they got a hold of my ankles, it was impossible to win the tug of war. They pulled me to the ground and handcuffed me.

WE'RE NOT GONNA TAKE IT - Twisted Sister

We're not gonna take it
No, we ain't gonna take it
We're not gonna take it anymore
We've got the right to choose, and
There ain't no way we'll lose it
This is our life, this is our song
We'll fight the powers that be, just
Don't pick on our destiny, 'cause
You don't know us, you don't belong
We're not gonna take it

No, we ain't gonna take it
We're not gonna take it anymore
Oh, you're so condescending
Your call is never ending
We don't want nothin', not a thing from you
Your life is trite and jaded
Boring and confiscated
If that's your best, your best won't do
Woah-oh-oh
Woah-oh-oh
We're right (yeah)
We're free (yeah)
We'll fight (yeah)
You'll see (yeah)

...

This led the crowd to begin chanting, "free speech," which got louder when they dragged me across the cobblestone patio. I went limp, forcing them to work harder at getting me to the police car in the distance on the other side of the parade ground. I remember holding my head up enough to not get knocked cold as they dragged me down the stairs to the grassy field. I was in shock enough that the bumps I took didn't hurt then, but I knew I would be bruised by morning.

The mob of students followed. Some ran ahead and gathered around the police car. When the policemen got me to the car, students were standing all around it. I grabbed the door handle with all my strength to resist being stuffed into the back seat.

One of the policemen punched me in the stomach hard enough to knock the wind out of me and break my resistance.

I recoiled enough to say, "Go ahead and beat me bloody. You'll just help my cause."

He knew I was right and hesitated long enough for a crowd of students to surround the car and stop the Police from taking me to Jail. I took advantage of the freedom, climbed onto the car, and continued speaking to the crowd.

"We will not be isolated any longer. We must destroy the administration's commitment to outside influences that make this university a place where the students' attitude is shaped by conformity and authority is not questioned. Students should not be trained to simply accept rules, bureaucracy, or justified circumstances."

There were miscellaneous cheers and shouting, "Right On, Free Speech."

"The establishment tells us that our future is not valid if we don't make money. That whatever else we do is meaningless. Well, hell, if this war continues, none of us will live to be thirty. So, we should live for the moment and judge ourselves by our own actions. We must find personal meaning in our lives before it's too late and we blow ourselves to hell."

There was a huge round of applause that progressed into a consolidated chanting. "Peace Now. Peace Now. Peace Now."

As nightfall came, the number of students grew to more than a thousand. Still successfully keeping from being stuffed into the Police car, the crowd of students stretched from around the police car to the Administration Building. More State Policemen had been mobilized, and many were motorcycle policemen.

While I was preaching from atop the police car, seemingly unrelated incidents were taking place around the freedom bell and inside the Administration Building. There were so many social and political issues erupting into protests and sit-ins that it was confusing what initiated the crowds being formed and what causes were represented; the draft, the Vietnam War, the Civil Rights movement, women's rights, and the sexual revolution, just to name a few. But the one common tone seemed to be impatience toward incremental change. Only signs carried by protesters gave identifying clues about a particular cause.

At nightfall, some students continued to ring the victory bell, while nearby, others removed the flag from the flagpole and lit it on fire.

LAY DOWN (CANDLES IN THE RAIN) –
Melanie Safka

Lay down, lay down, lay it all down
Let your white birds smile up at the ones who stand and frown
Lay down, lay down, lay it all down
Let your white birds smile up at the ones who stand and frown

We were so close, there was no room
We bled inside each other's wounds
We all had caught the same disease
And we all sang the songs of peace
Lay down, lay down, lay it all down
Let your white birds smile up at the ones who stand and frown
Lay down, lay down, lay it all down

Let your white birds smile up at the ones who stand and
frown
So raise the candles high
'Cause if you don't, we could stay black against the night
Oh, raise them higher again
And if you do, we could stay dry against the rain

...

Inside the administration building, the hallway was
jammed with more than a hundred students. There was
sort of a festive air about it. There were posters on the walls,
peace signs, and slogans: Down With The Establishment,
Don't Trust Anyone Over Thirty, and Hell No We Won't
Go.

Some female students had removed all their clothes to
liberate themselves from the confining conventions of life,
while others were lying on sleeping bags laughing and
socializing. The 4-H club was making peanut butter and
jelly sandwiches. A committee organized to create an
alternative curriculum in a far corner was getting students
to sign petitions. Some students were rolling and passing
around joints. Some others were sitting around bubbling
bongs and taking tokes.

Professor Hadsell was there, huddled with a few other
faculty members. They had been taking everybody's name
down, not just those directly participating in any
obstruction activity, and Hadsell was compiling them.

Then, with the compiled list, the Professor, with the
trailing group of teachers, marched into the Dean's Office
and presented the list to the Dean.

"This is a complete list of all students in the building that
we can identify. "Most gave their names voluntarily, and
some even signed the lists directly." said Hadsell as he

resentfully dropped the list on the Dean's desk. "You asshole!" Hadsell said in a subdued voice.

"Okay," said the Dean, pretending not to hear the Professor, "Now that some of the agitators are identified, we can divide and conquer."

Hadsell was agitated and tense. "Do you realize that several thousand students outside are prepared to take their place? You can't throw them all off-campus; there wouldn't be anybody left to teach!"

The Dean reached for the phone. We're not going to do anything." "Get me the Governor," he said into the phone.

"I will say whatever it takes to get them to disperse for the night. By tomorrow morning, the National Guard will swarm this campus like flies on a horse's ass."

Professor Hadsell turned back at the door as he was leaving. "By the way, I've also put my name on the list!"

The Dean reacted with a glare to Hadsell's insolence as the phone rang, connecting him with the Governor.

"Then I guess your work on this campus is finished, Professor."

"Governor," he said into the phone, "how's everything in Santa Fe? Good. Say, Dave, I've run into a problem here and need to take some precautionary measures."

The National Guard had now been officially requested.

Later in the hallway, the Dean addressed the students using a bullhorn.

"Weldon Sipe will be booked and released tomorrow on his own recognizance."

Some of the crowd booed.

"And then, all charges against him will be dropped." Some cheered.

Tommy showed no fear of asking questions. "What about free speech on the campus."

"A committee to resolve these issues will be set up with representatives of the students, including leaders of the SDS, and representatives of the faculty and administration."

"What about the free speech area?" Tommy shouted.

"I see no reason why we can't restore public forum but with some guidelines," spoke the Dean.

Noises from the crowd indicated some were satisfied, some were questioning, and others were not satisfied.

"We have an agreement then," said the Dean. "The demonstration is over. Please leave in an orderly fashion, and let's get the campus back to normal. Good night."

He made his way to his office with the Assistant Dean following.

At the door, he turned to the Assistant.

"Change the suspension charges to permanent expulsion for everyone who was cited last week. Send letters to everyone on the list that there will be a disciplinary hearing."

Across the parade ground, the State Policemen were implementing their plan. They had set up two rows of motorcycles and pulled the students out between the two rows as they worked their way toward the surrounded police car. Finally, they created a pathway, pulled me from atop the police car, and drove me to jail. I was angry but more tired, worn out, and sore from being dragged down the stairs and across the parade field.

Professor Hadsell came to visit me at the County Jail. He seemed very personable but still maintained a teacher mindset. "They think we have given up," I stated.

"Yes, but the administration won't give up the right to discipline any student who was involved," said Hadsell. "And that's exactly what they are going to do."

"I didn't mean to get you fired," I said to shift the subject.

"Oh well," he said. "I felt a real obligation to those students, and now I will just have to find a real job." He stood up and extended his hand. "Good luck, Weldon.

"Yes, good luck," I replied, shaking his hand.

"I only hope that historians won't record these times as just some fashion statement about hippies, beads, and music," Hadsell said.

"History based on written records is only five percent true. You said so," I reminded him.

"Yes," he said. "And the remaining truth is lost through the rewriting of history. Then eventually, it will appear to have been all for nothing."

"I'll try not to let that happen," I said, "if I have to write the story myself."

The Professor left. I was only momentarily alone when Ginny came to my cell.

"Weldon?" I turned toward her but did not speak. I had nothing to say.

"I moved out," she said with a barely audible voice. "I'm going back home."

I had nothing to say.

"I'll be gone by the time you get out of jail." I still had nothing to say.

Suddenly she started sobbing. "Oh, Weldon, William is dead!" I was stunned. "What?" I joined her at the jail bars.

"He was killed a few days ago on a routine patrol. There wasn't supposed to be any enemy around."

"I'm sorry, Gin. You know I am." Ginny managed to stop sobbing.

"They're shipping his body back by Army transport, and it could be a week or even longer."

There was nothing for me to say.

"I never meant this to happen," she said. "I was just trying to reach you somehow, to let you know I was lonely."

I thought she wanted forgiveness, but I wasn't ready to offer it. "Weldon?" She sensed that forgiveness wasn't forthcoming.

"You didn't have to betray me," I blurted out.

Then, after an uncomfortable pause, she turned and was gone.

Chapter 29

THE RESERVE OFFICERS TRAINING CORPS

While I was in jail, the National Guard rolled onto the college campus with various armored trucks and vehicles loaded with troops dressed in riot gear.

Behind the Reserve Officers Training Corps (ROTC) Building, three students stood in front of a rear window.

"Why don't we just trash the place and leave it at that?" said one of them.

"Hey man, come on," replied another. "They're keeping files on us in there and giving information to the draft board. Let's just do it."

Suddenly he threw a rock he had been holding through a window. The first student held up a small torch, and the other lit it with a cigarette lighter and tossed it through the broken window.

When I was finally released from jail, I went back to the campus to find the entrance road totally impassable. I parked my car in the same place I had spent hours atop a police car the night before. The campus was in chaos. The National Guard troops were everywhere, some marching, some on rooftops, and some standing by armored vehicles awaiting orders. The ROTC building was in flames, and the fire department could only contain the blaze.

Many students rallied at the freedom bell in opposition to the military presence on campus.

They chanted, "One, two, three, four, we don't want your fucking war."

It seemed out of nowhere that the crowd at the freedom bell swelled to over a thousand, and every time the freedom bell was rung, it beckoned for even more students to come.

A smaller faction of the group began chanting, "Pigs off campus. Pigs off campus."

The atmosphere was tense with the sudden influx of so many students. A campus policeman rode shotgun in a National Guard jeep ordering the crowd using a bullhorn.

"I order you to disperse and go home. All you bystanders and innocent people go home for your own safety."

This whipped the students into a further frenzy. I joined the group of students at the bell. After all, this was our campus. Except for the ROTC fire, we all thought we were doing nothing wrong. They had no right to order us to disperse; if anyone should be leaving, it shouldn't be the students.

OHIO - Neil Young

Tin soldiers and Nixon coming
We're finally on our own
This summer I hear the drumming
Four dead in Ohio
Gotta get down to it, soldiers are cutting
us down
Should have been gone long ago
What if you knew her and found her dead on the ground
How can you run when you know?

La-la-la-la, la-la-la-la
La-la-la-la, la-la-la
La-la-la-la, la-la-la-la
La-la-la-la, la-la-la

Gotta get down to it, soldiers are cutting us down
Should have been gone long ago
What if you knew her and found her dead on the ground
How can you run when you know?
Tin soldiers and Nixon coming
We're finally on our own
This summer I hear the drumming
Four dead in Ohio

...

These were confusing times. This protest had many issues—if it was still just a protest. Its purpose suddenly changed when a violent student flung a bottle at a National Guard jeep that splattered on the side. This, of course, alarmed the jeep's occupants, so they hurriedly drove off toward a National Guard line that had formed in the distance and in front of the remains of the smoldering ROTC building. This started what became more like a war every minute it continued, and a chain reaction of events commenced.

The National Guardsmen leveled their bayonets at us. They started to march across in our direction, shooting tear gas as they advanced. In an instant, the situation became severe. We were either going to be gassed, stabbed, or both. My knees were shaking, and my heart was thumping. Students scattered in all directions. The teargas reached us before the troops did. My eyes started watering and burning, and my vision became blurred. I was helpless. So, I chose to rush from the area along with many others. A few delayed leaving and threw tear-gas canisters back at the soldiers, which was ludicrous because they were wearing gas masks. I retreated to what I thought was a safe distance thinking that the soldiers would leave after seeing the students scatter. Still, instead, they kept advancing until they caught up with some of them.

Three students were surrounded, and to my horror, they were being forced to lie on the ground. One of the students was bent over and vomiting. Not listening to the soldiers' demands to lie down, he raised his hands overhead to show surrender and was bayoneted.

The soldiers continued advancing in my direction, and I was no longer a safe distance away. I ran to the girl's dormitory, where some resident students had opened the windows, were passing out water to clear our throats, and moistened paper towels to wipe our burning eyes. Suddenly they were screaming and slamming their windows closed. I looked toward the National Guard, and they were close but suddenly turned and proceeded back toward the remains of the ROTC building.

I was relieved but still had to wipe my eyes to see. The National Guardsmen were surrounded on all sides by students. Curiously, I moved closer to watch. Some students were throwing rocks at the National Guard, and some of the National Guard were picking up the rocks and throwing them back at the students.

The students got closer and closer to the retreating Guardsmen and threw more rocks and canisters of tear gas back at them. Momentarily, the Guardsmen huddled into a group. Suddenly, they turned with bayonets and pointed them at the students. Some students followed close behind. I cautiously moved even closer to a small group of trees. There were other onlookers around me.

The National Guardsmen turned in a quick flurry and bayoneted some of the students closest to them. I saw the bayoneted students on the ground as the other students scattered.

Without further provocation, the Guardsmen began advancing and firing their rifles. Students screamed, and more students fell victim to the Guardsmen. These few seconds seemed an eternity.

Tears were streaming down one Guardsman's face. He was advancing as he was told, and suddenly he dropped to his knees to protest the atrocity.

"Oh my God!" he said. "They are just kids!"

A nearby Guardsman quickly pulled the kneeling soldier to his feet by his shirt.

"Get up!" he yelled. "You signed up for this. Now do as you're told."

The students' parted, moving to one side or the other to let the Guardsmen pass. No one in their right mind stood there as bayonets and firing rifles advanced.

Everything seemed to be in slow motion when I turned to run. I only made it a step or two when I heard two cracks of rifle fire above all the rest of the noise. I felt a sharp pain in my foot, and my shoe flew into the air. I was knocked off my feet and into the air and fell to the ground with a thud. From the corner of my eye, I saw a bone sticking through my sock.

My head hit the ground, and my body became limp and motionless. I could still see soldiers moving about, so I knew I was not dead. I tried to raise myself, but I couldn't.

Amid the screams and commotion, I heard someone yelling, "Stay down! Stay down!"

I looked in the direction of the voice, back toward the trees. It was Bud behind a tree.

Reality set in. I was caught in an open area and unable to run. I lay there as prone as possible to shield myself from the gunfire. The bullets were hitting within inches of my head. I could see students farther down the hill dropping, some hit, some just hugging the ground.

I put my hands over my ears to drown out the screaming from the wounded and the fleeing. It seemed like an eternity, and I let out a shriek, "STOOOOOOOOOOOOP."

Swiftly I was being lifted. Bud had picked me up like a sack of potatoes and threw me over his shoulder. He was carrying me as fast as he could, my head downward. We passed a girl's lifeless body.

Then another shot went off and Bud groaned. I knew he must have been shot as he almost dropped me, but he kept going. Blood was dripping down my arm onto the ground, and I did not know if it was Bud's or mine. I blacked out.

I woke up slowly, looking at the ceiling and hearing ambulance sirens, doors slamming, people running, and gurneys being wheeled up and down a hall. I finally remembered what had happened. I quickly sat up to see if my foot was still there, and the tips of my toes were sticking out of a cast. With a sigh of relief, I laid back down, feeling like I was about ready to black out again when I noticed Bud was sitting beside my bed, and his arm was in a sling.

"Why don't you look at the odds before you get into a fight?" he said.

I managed to muster a smile and hold up my fist as a sign of the power of protest. Then I blacked out.

When I came to, the TV in my room was on. News clips depicted the growing numbers of protests nationwide and emotional footage of civil disobedience, such as the burning of draft cards and candlelight gatherings. The newscaster said 500,000 protesters had demonstrated in Washington following a nationwide moratorium against the war.

And finally, there was newsreel footage of the gunning down of students by National Guardsmen at Kent State University in Ohio, where 4 were killed and 9 wounded.

Bud drove me back to the University in his truck when I was released.

"OK," I asked, "How did you get me out of jail?"

"Well, it must have looked bad to keep students in jail for exercising their right to free speech. So, they set bail low enough that I could raise enough to cover it," he replied.

"Where did you get the money?"

"You remember the gang that harassed us at the bar?" I nodded yes.

"Well, they tried to get a rise out of me several days ago by asking what happened to my sidekick. So, I just told them what had happened. The next thing I knew, they passed a cowboy hat around, taking up a collection. They were stunned that you and me were dumb enough to take on the whole U.S. government."

As we came upon the school entrance, some students were driving out cars loaded with furniture and personal belongings. A big sign was posted at the arch: THIS CAMPUS IS CLOSED UNTIL NEXT SEMESTER. ALL CLASSES HAVE BEEN SUSPENDED.”

We continued driving through the university, looking around at the riot’s aftermath. National Guardsmen were posted at every building, and signs said the buildings were closed. FBI had marked off areas with barrier tape where students were killed, taking pictures and looking for evidence. The local police were picking up rocks and tear gas canisters thrown during the riot. Bulldozers were beginning to clear the burned- out ROTC building.

At the victory bell, there were more National Guardsmen. They allowed student mourners to congregate, weep, light candles, and place flowers around the bell. One girl stuffed a flower down the barrel of a nearby soldier’s rifle, and he did not flinch.

Bud got our mail at the campus post office and handed me a letter when he got back into the truck. I opened it, and it was from the War Resisters League.

We arrived at the dorm, I on crutches, and Bud with his arm in a sling.

“What are you going to do now?” I asked.

“I don’t really know,” he said. “Punch cows and mend fences, I guess. And drink a few beers, too. I’ll be back when classes start. How about you?”

“First, I got a showdown with the draft board. Then we’ll see after that.” Then as an afterthought, “Think I can punch cows?”

Bud gave me a sarcastic look. "I didn't think so," I responded.

"You can tip a few beers, though," he said. "Why don't we stop by Dicks? I'd like to see your face turn red one more time."

I didn't know it then, but this would be the last I would ever see Bud. I wonder from time to time what happened to him or if he is still alive.

Chapter 30
ON THE ROAD AGAIN

It was late afternoon when I finished packing what few things would fit in my VW and started my long road trip to Pennsylvania through Carlsbad. Tommy, who was acquainted with Buck, told me that Buck was married to a woman named Marilee and was from Carlsbad. I figured I had some unfinished business with Buck's wife, Marilee. I hoped to understand what happened between Ginny and me and what drove her to be unfaithful. Talking with Marilee just might do that.

When I arrived in Carlsbad, it was too late for a visit seeing that it was early evening and Buck might be there. I checked into a fleabag motel. After staring at the walls for an hour, I contacted her by telephone. I had many expectations, including assuming she was home and amicable about talking with me. I was very anxious about the call. The phone rang quite a few times. I was about to hang up when she answered it.

"Hello?"

"Marilee Walls?" I asked. "Yes?" she replied cautiously.

"My name is Weldon Sipe...and...I...."

"Look, if you're another bill collector, I don't have any money. You'll have to see Buck. He's the only one who knows where it all goes."

"No, I'm not a bill collector," I said. "This is a personal matter."

"Do I know you?" she said warily.

"No. Your husband and my wife are having an affair."
She didn't speak right away. The suspense was killing me.

Finally, she spoke. "I wouldn't doubt it. You're not the
first if that makes you feel any better."

"No. It doesn't." I remained silent to allow what I had
just heard to sink in.

"I'm sorry. Buck makes his rounds around this town."

"Well, I'm not from this town," I said. "I'm from Las
Cruces, well I was until...."

"He's been way over there?" asked Marilee. "Yes."

Silence again.

"I'm really sorry, Weldon. Really, I am." "Mrs. Walls, I
just..."

"Marilee," she inserted. "Just call me Marilee."

This was a good sign. We were now on a first-name
basis.

"Marilee," I responded. "Please. Let me visit and talk
with you. I promise not to take up a lot of your time."

"Well, OK. But if he catches me, he'll...." I could hear a
door slamming behind her.

"I'm back," said Buck in the distance.

Marilee cut our conversation short. "Sorry, but I'm not
interested and can't afford it."

Quickly I added, "I'm staying at the Good Knight Motel.
Come if..."

"Goodbye," she said as she hung up.

I paced the floor for several hours. My mind was racing with thoughts, like, what am I doing here? What did I expect to accomplish? I knew I wanted revenge for having my devotion and honor crushed. I was furious, and the angrier I became as the time passed. I was always available to her, even during the day and between classes.

I couldn't remember the last time Ginny initiated having sex. It seemed she was okay with just submitting to my advances to get what she must have perceived as her obligation over with.

My thoughts turned to Marilee.

Apparently, after waiting several hours, Marilee wasn't coming, so I went to bed.

I woke up in what seemed to be the middle of the night to a faint knocking at my motel room door. Peeking through the window curtain, I was surprised to see a woman I assumed was Marilee. I opened the door.

"I didn't think you were coming," I said.

She was only in silhouette from the outside light. I reached to turn on the light on the table lamp.

"Leave it off," she said.

"OK," I complied.

"Do you mind if I freshen up? Every time he touches me, I feel I need a bath."

"No, of course not," I said. "Is he still at home waiting for you?"

"No, he's gone. Probably won't be back until his shift starts at the mine on Monday. He's gone to meet up with some female somewhere, I'm sure. Maybe your wife, for all I know."

"I wouldn't know," I affirmed. "We've separated, and I moved into the dormitory."

"Probably for the best," she said as she finished removing all but her panties. She went into the bathroom and turned on the shower water, feeling it with her hand and waiting for it to warm up. The light in the bathroom lit her body, and my heart started pounding. God, she was beautiful. Her athletic body was muscular and shapely, and her skin was white like buttermilk.

Anticipating sex, it felt the same as I had during my first time with Ginny in the back seat of my Volkswagen. My legs were quivering with excitement. Were we going to get revenge for our cheating spouses without telling our stories to each other and embellishing them with lies to admonish any feeling of guilt about what we were about to do? Or did she only want to freshen up, as she said?

I couldn't take my eyes off her. There was only one way to find out which outcome it would be. I took off my robe and my underwear and cautiously entered the bathroom. What was the worst that would happen? She would get angry, put on her clothes, and storm out the door. I watched her through the see-through curtain. She was bent forward, rigorously scrubbing her vagina with a washcloth. I was sexually aroused. I wanted revenge, and I wanted her.

Slowly, I pulled back the plastic curtain. She turned and looked at me but did not say a word. Then, I noticed she had a bruised cheek and a blackened eye. Still, with her bruises, Marilee was a strikingly beautiful young woman with long copper-red hair and exquisite feminine features.

I stepped in and put my arms around her. The nipples of her breasts pressed against me. She suddenly turned her back toward me.

"Scrub my back," she said.

It was then that I realized that she was in charge of the situation. She was orchestrating my every move. My cock was throbbing, and I did what she said. Following the curve of her torso to her ass, I couldn't resist pressing my shaft into her crack. She pressed back, wedging me deeper. She was alluring, mysterious, and totally vulnerable.

"Fuck me," she said softly.

She wanted me. All of me. Right now. She expressed her wild streak, and I rose to the opportunity.

This was more than just revenge for her lousy marriage. She wanted something more. I had never had ass sex before, but I had friends that talked about it. The possibility was fascinating to me. The thought of feeling her butt cheeks slapping against my thighs and her butthole around my dick was incredibly empowering. And now the opportunity was here to express my desire to feel dominant, to have ownership over Marilee like I never did over Ginny.

I looked at her ass. "You are so beautiful," I said in a soft voice. The fact that she would allow me rear entry was already very enticing. I couldn't imagine anything more intimate.

I started to rub the shaft of my penis up and down between the cheeks of her ass.

"Go easy," she whispered.

Even though I hadn't had this experience before, I knew instinctively not to shove my cock into her. But the way she whispered to me was more informative than fearful. I was concerned for her possible pain despite my intense desire, which was like a roller coaster ride between eagerness, anxiety, and pleasure. When trying to insert the head of my penis, I realized it was a challenge to penetrate her sphincter. It took me a few tries, but finally, she relaxed enough that it broke through. When it did, she took a quick breath.

"That feels good," she murmured.

I couldn't imagine what that felt like for her.

I began taking little strokes, gradually going deeper and deeper until I was pretty far inside.

"That feels good," she repeated, followed by a few moans.

I increased the intensity of my strokes. It felt like nothing I'd experienced before, like I had never had sex before.

Soon all I could think about was the pressure against my prostate from the tightness of her sphincter muscle that made me harder than ever. The pleasantly luxurious feeling continued to build to my ejaculation. She was now moaning and moving in rhythm with my strokes.

"Don't stop," she said, but it was too late.

I soon came so hard that the electrified sensation radiated through my whole body. Marilee's verbal commands kept my erection hard, and I kept going. Her moaning got louder and louder. Then she suddenly held her breath and started quivering. Finally, she exhaled peacefully into a resting state.

We cuddled in bed for a while, knowing our relationship was just a one-night stand. Not that I wouldn't want it to continue, but we both had things in our lives that needed to be resolved. She laid her head on my chest, and I stroked her hair. It was the most intimate sex of my life.

"Marilee," I finally said, "Things aren't going to get any better, you know."

She didn't respond.

"You need to leave him."

Chapter 31
THE CENTRAL COMMITTEE FOR CONSCIENTIOUS OBJECTORS

I drove all the way to Philadelphia invigorated by the high from having a memorable and completely satisfying sexual experience. I stopped only once to rest my eyes for an hour or two.

I finally reached the Central Committee for Conscientious Objectors (CCCO) headquarters. I found it housed in the intercity area. It was mainly office buildings with traditional Pennsylvania architecture consisting of red brick encased in cement and windows under brick archways.

I received a copy of 'THE HANDBOOK FOR CONSCIENTIOUS OBJECTORS' when I moved into the dormitory. A lot had happened since then, and I did not expect they could reverse my draft notice. Still, they supported conscientious objectors and promoted resistance to this war and all other wars, including preparations for war. It was the only source that provided complete and accurate information about the process I had initiated.

I entered with an open mind, anxious to understand my choices because I was already drafted. The draft counselor seemed tired and overworked but attentive enough. Within a minute, we were down to the earnest questions.

"Let me understand you more clearly?" he asked. "You are opposed to the Vietnam War?"

"No sir," I replied emphatically. "I am opposed to all war."

"Okay," he said, meaning I had said something that qualified for further discussion. "Let me get some background. When did you discover that you were a conscientious objector?"

"My discovery has evolved in recent months becoming obvious to me while I worked on nuclear submarines. At first, I was proud but began to feel ashamed that I was part of some sort of military-industrial insanity. I was unfamiliar with the term conscientious objector. In fact, I had never heard of the term until I became a graduate school student in Political Science. Once I became familiar with it, I identified with it. Like most other graduate students, I felt I had to face the problem head-on in my own way. The shit hit the fan when they started taking student deferments away from graduate students. You see if I am forced into the military now, I will not complete my basic required courses within the allotted time and will have to start all over again."

"So, what is your game plan?"

"I have no game plan. I am here to know my options."

"So, you're not opposed to entering the military, just not at this time?"

"No, sir. Look, I will not go into the military no matter what the outcome of this process. I will not cooperate with the draft."

"Are you opposed to military service because of religious beliefs?"

"No," I replied

"Political, moral, or humanitarian grounds?"

"No, not really, well yes," I said to all three, "but I feel that I lack the ability to explain or defend myself."

The counselor sat back in his chair. "You have chosen a difficult road to travel. In fact, the most difficult. Have you been requested to appear before your local board?"

"Yes," I replied.

"Good. That's good. We have to exhaust all avenues of possibilities within the law first. So then, let's get you prepared for your hearing. I want you to follow these 10 rules."

Then he began, "Number 1. Everything must be in writing, keep copies, and send us copies. We can't advise you on the best course of action if we don't know what's happening, and most often, we can't help you if it is long after things occur. Number 2. Know what you believe and be prepared to explain it clearly and concisely. Practice expressing yourself orally and in writing. It will be an emotionally charged atmosphere. They are going to take procedural liberties, but you cannot. Many sincere conscientious objectors are in prison because of carelessness or ignorance of the law or the process."

I listened carefully to him for the next several hours and asked very few questions, and I felt good every time he used the word "we" while talking. He gave me a lot to think about, and I certainly revised my thinking because of his instruction. It would be more academic and more antagonistic than I had imagined. Still, the CCCO counselor made me feel that I was not alone. My copy of the Handbook for Conscientious Objectors became my bible.

Chapter 32
EXPLAINING IT TO MOTHER

My relationship with my mother became indifferent since my marriage to Ginny. She was happy that I had married into money, but she didn't think we were a good match. After all, they were Catholics and, worse, Italian Catholics. She wanted nothing to do with people like that. She despised their religion and their ethnicity.

Our relationship had improved from awkward to nonchalant after I told her I was home because the University was temporarily closed due to the riots. I informed my mother that I had an upcoming meeting with my draft board in Greensburg concerning my student deferment. She usually kept out of my business and only asked questions when her curiosity got the best of her. She always started a conversation with a sarcastic remark that asserted her viewpoint. She thought she was amusing when she pointed out the weaknesses of people.

I was writing a 10-page thesis about what it meant to me to be a conscientious objector as a practice for what may be asked at my Local Board hearing. This was one of the to-do list suggestions I got from the CCCO.

Mother came into the living room where I was writing the thesis and said, "I don't understand what you're hearing with the Local Board is about."

"You remember me telling you I received my draft notice?" She nodded that she remembered.

"I'm trying to get reclassified 1-0,"

As soon as I had said this, I realized by the expression on her face that she really didn't have a clue what that meant.

"The classification 1-0 means that I am conscientiously opposed to all wars."

"You mean the Vietnam War?" she questioned.

"No. All wars. This hearing, which I requested, is not specifically about the Vietnam War. It is my legal right to challenge the classification by proving to them that I am a conscientious objector."

"What if they don't agree to reclassify you?"

Rather than go into a long explanation, I said, "It really doesn't matter. I'm not going."

"You know your father would not agree with you if he were alive. He was very patriotic."

"I don't know if we would even be on speaking terms, but that doesn't matter now. I have to do this. If all legal avenues fail, then its jail or Canada. Jail is a 5-year sentence, and Canada means I can never come back to this country. Either way, the only way I can get out of this war is civil disobedience, meaning to be a conscientious objector."

"Maybe Uncle Frank can give you some advice? He understands the military and I'm not sure I understand all this."

"Honestly mother, I don't give a damn what Frank thinks"

"Weldon! I Guess I just don't understand you. I don't know where you get your ideas. What will people think? I have to live here you know?"

Chapter 33

ABOUT MY UNCLE FRANK

My Uncle Frank was a career soldier. He enlisted right out of high school when we were at war. He hated the Japanese and had maybe just a smidgen of respect for the Germans, and all others were just sub- human. And since they were not within the human race, it was okay to kill as many as possible, including women and children, as they would breed more sub-humans. He completed 33 bombing missions over Germany toward the war's end, and his plane was shot down three times. One of those times, he was the only survivor. That made him a hero, according to many people.

If you called him a hero, he would snap back, "I'm not a hero. The only heroes I know are dead. The survivors of the war need not be recognized. They were just doing the job they signed up to do."

There was another side to Uncle Frank that no one seemed to understand. We never talked about what he did. I think he carried a burden of unresolved feelings of guilt about what he must have seen and probably did. One time, when he was drunk and got very gloomy, he commented that he didn't want to think about how many schools, hospitals, and innocent people and children were killed by the exploding bombs he was dropping. It was killing him inside. He was emotionally numb and felt spiritually rejected. He never went to church and was certain of going to hell, as he would say once in a while. His constant abuse of alcohol was his way of numbing those feelings and memories. Most people wanted to praise him for his service. While drunk, people would avoid conversation with him,

213

and that was probably what he wanted. Being a military lifer, he always portrayed a persona of being combat-ready. He could stand at perfect attention while drunk and talked almost like he was giving orders.

Before his death, he told my mother he wanted to be buried in his military uniform because "Being a soldier was all I ever did. I want to die like one."

He insisted that he be buried in his moth-eaten uniform in an Eisenhower special, a plain metal casket.

"What was good enough for General Eisenhower is good enough for me."

I think in his mind being buried like other soldiers gave him a glimmer of possible salvation because he wasn't the only one to commit such atrocities.

My mother continued with her questions.

"What are they going to do at this hearing? I mean, what are you expecting them to do?"

"Well, they will listen to me state my position, ask questions, and then after the meeting, they will discuss my position on the matter and inform me by mail of their decision. If their decision is unanimous, then that's the end of it, and the draft notice stands."

"And then I suppose you will go into the military?"

"No. I have already told you that I won't go into the military, no matter what the outcome of this hearing. I am just exercising all possible legal avenues first to avoid military service."

"What does Ginny say about all this?"

"She left me, Mother. She has no say."

CHAPTER 34
WILLIAM'S FUNERAL

Mother had received a call from Ginny's mother telling her that she was welcome at the funeral for Willie. She told me about the phone call and informed me that she would not attend because she was opposed to our marriage and wasn't invited to our wedding. With what little respect I had left for Ginny, I felt I should attend Willie's funeral.

The funeral service was concluding when I arrived at the cemetery. I drove up in my Volkswagen and stood in the background. Near me were several soldiers from Willie's National Guard unit. There was a small color guard, and it was impressive enough. I was carrying a lot of anger, and I thought it was toward Ginny until I started walking over to the grave site. With every step, my anger toward Ginny subsided and shifted to the military pretentiousness that death was far more valued than life itself.

Ginny watched the flag being folded and looked overwhelmed by the pomp and circumstance of the ceremony. It meant more to the military than to her. Obviously, she was not at peace over Willie's death.

I overheard one soldier telling the other, "The next thing I knew, we were in Vietnam. Six of us, including Willie, were sent into the jungle just before Christmas. We weren't there 30 seconds when the fighting started, and Willie was shot in the head."

The color guard handed the folded flag to Maureen, who could not hold back her tears. Earl was grieving but maintained his Italian toughness facade through the ceremony.

Ginny peered at me, bewildered, as I joined them. She would not move toward me as I expected, but Earl did once he spotted me. I knew that he wasn't going to be pleasant.

"You have no right to be here," he huffed. "You're not part of this family anymore."

"I understand how you feel," I countered, "but…."

"No, you don't," Earl said insistently, "If it wasn't for commie pinkos like you, we could lick those gook bastards."

"This isn't my war, and it wasn't William's either," I replied.

"William did his part, which is more than I can say for you. He did his patriotic duty. God rest his soul."

"He tried to beat the system just like everybody else," I said, countering. "It just didn't work out, that's all."

"He wasn't no draft dodger like you, and don't start insinuating he was."

Unknowingly I had lit his fuse. "If I could, I'd send your sorry ass over there today, but it wouldn't do us any good. Look at ya. You look like a hippie bum. If we weren't in front of all these people, I'd shove that peace symbol that's around your neck up your ass."

I tried to remain calm.

"We can't win this war. What do you want? You want to slaughter them until the last poor rice farmer stands in the middle of his rice patty, defying you as you kill him, too?"

"Damn right," said Earl. "Smash his fuckin flat face right into his rice bowl until he chokes on it."

"Might makes right, uh?"

"Might makes right!"

"And what did you get for it? Fat money because war is good business. Oh, and this, of course,"

I pointed to the military gravestones.

"There are millions of little white markers just like them."

For the moment, Earl was speechless. I glanced over at Ginny, and she was looking at me with an expression somewhere between condemnation and admiration.

"You know I would have stopped him from going if I could," I said to her. "You know that Gin."

Maureen cried out with loud sobs. Earl went to console her. "Just leave Weldon. Leave us alone."

"I've been drafted," I said at once. Tears immediately formed in her eyes as she came closer to me.

"I asked for a hearing for conscientious objector status, but I don't expect it will change things."

I pulled a letter from my pocket and handed it to her. "I've made some other arrangements if I'm rejected."

Ginny read the letter. It was from the War Resisters League and addressed to me. It read, "Meet me at the Niagara border on June 26. Bring 300 US dollars cash as required to file for permanent residency. I will help you fill out the forms at the border and vouch for your employment here. Sincerely, Jutsie."

"To Canada?!"

"If it's the only choice, I'll take it."

"But you can never come back!" she said chocked up.

I looked away toward the hundreds of white military markers, all in rows.

"Neither can they."

We stood there staring at the rows and rows of markers. It was one of those awkward moments that stayed with me for the rest of my life.

I AIN'T MARCHING ANYMORE - Phil Ochs

Oh, I marched to the battle of New Orleans
At the end of the early British wars
The young land started growing
The young blood started flowing
But I ain't marching anymore
For I've killed my share of Indians
In a thousand different fights
I was there at the Little Big Horn
I heard many men lying, I saw many more dying
But I ain't marching anymore

It's always the old to lead us to the wars
It's always the young to fall
Now look at all we've won with the saber and the gun
Tell me, is it worth it all?

For I stole California from the Mexican land
Fought in the bloody Civil War
Yes, I even killed my brothers
And so many others
But I ain't marching anymore

For I marched to the battles ofthe German trench
In a war that was bound to end all wars
Oh, I must have killed a million men
And now they want me back again
But I ain't marching anymore

It's always the old to lead us to the wars
Always the young to fall
Now look at all we've won with the saber and the gun
Tell me, is it worth it all?

For I flew the final mission in the Japanese skies
Set off the mighty mushroom roar

When I saw the cities burning
I knew that I was learning
That I ain't marching anymore
Now the labor leader's screamin'
When they close the missile plants
United Fruit screams at the Cuban shore
Call it peace or call it treason
Call it love or call it reason
But I ain't marching anymore
No, I ain't marching anymore

There was nothing more to say. Other funerals were
going on or being prepared. A color guard was already
forming at the cemetery entrance gate for the next burial.

CHAPTER 35
GOD'S ON OUR SIDE?

I went to see the pastor of our family church where I was baptized. It was just before the church service, and Reverend Murdock looked at my draft board meeting notice.

"I need your support," I said to Reverend Murdock. It would surely help to have your support."

"Well, Weldon, officially, the church has no position."

I knew the Reverend was generally unclear on all matters, especially anything affecting his standing with the congregation.

"Sure, it has," I said. "We are to live according to the example set by Jesus Christ, aren't we?"

"Well, yes, of course, but this is the real world," he responsed as he began gathering loose papers together for his sermon.

"And his era wasn't?"

"You know what I mean, Weldon. We must be practical."

"The events of his life were a set-up for his words," I tried to clarify. "Words for his ideals that are not really attainable by us. Is that it?"

"I understand how you feel, Weldon, but if every young man believed as you, then we may as well turn ourselves over to our enemies and be done with it."

"So, praise the Lord but pass the ammunition then."

"Don't be disrespectful now," he said, being short with me because his service was about to begin.

"Let me ask you this, in your wildest imagination, would you have ever thought that Jesus would enlist in the military?"

"Of course not," he said abruptly.

"Did he ever point out any exceptions to "Thou Shall Not Kill?" The Reverend was irritated. I was irritated even more.

"Let's see if I can get this straight. Jesus Christ would never join the military and become an instrument of death because to kill was a violation of God's commandments. In fact, he told us that if our enemy were to slap us on the cheek, we are to let him slap the other cheek also. And when he's done kicking us in the ass, we are to hug and tell him we love him. I have it basically right, don't I? It's a simple message, or is there something I don't understand?"

The organ started playing the prelude to the service. The Reverend got up and headed for the door to the pulpit.

"I don't have any more time for this discussion," he said.

"Look, Reverend, I'm not saying that we shouldn't bring justice to wrongdoings, and I'm not asking you to argue my position. All I am asking is that you appear at the meeting. Stand beside me, that is all. Support my seeking justice according to the law."

"I'll do what I can," he said as he shut the door behind him. "I have to go."

Heading toward the sanctuary exit, I passed the organ cubicle where Howard, the church organist, sat.

"Hey, Howard. How's it hanging?"

"Not too well," he said. "I thought I was going to Julliard, but I've been drafted."

"Bummer," I said. "What are you going to do?"

"What do ya think?" Howard responded remorsefully.

"You don't have to go. I'm not."

"How did you get out ofit?"

"I didn't, yet. I have a hearing tomorrow."

"Really? Claiming 1-A-0?"

"No 1-0."

"1-0! Wow, you got guts. I was thinking of shooting myself in the foot or something."

"If more don't stand up, nothing will change," I said.

"That may be so, but I don't like picking up soap in the prison shower for five years, if you know what I mean."

"I was hoping Reverend Murdock ...."

"Don't count on the Reverend," Howard responded. "He has to answer to the silent majority, you know. Officially the church may coo like a dove, but most of this congregation flies like hawks."

He looked at his watch, turned to the organ keyboard, and began playing. "Keep me posted, eh Weldon?"

"Don't forget to let me know how you like Julliard."

I didn't stay for the service but stood outside the church listening to Howard play. I felt like the church had turned its back on me. Reverend Murdock soon started speaking from the pulpit.

"Today, it is with great pride and yet with sadness that I announce that Howard Sapier will leave us in a few days to serve our country in the armed forces. We praise him, and all others who choose to enter the military, and we will surely miss him." He turned toward the organ cubicle. "Howard? Would you like to come out and play something special for us today? Howard, would you do that while we collect the morning offering?"

Howard came into the sanctuary, and the congregation applauded. "Great! Wonderful," exclaimed Murdock with pride.

Howard walked over to the piano at the front of the sanctuary. In reference to the cold war, an American flag decorated the piano. He sat down, put his music in place, and then turned on the microphone. The audience was so proud. At the last moment, Howard decided not to play what he had planned before beginning to play. He closed the music and began playing something different, something that was on his mind. Howard started singing.

WITH GOD ON OUR SIDE - Manfred Mann

My name it is nothing, my age it means less
The country I come from is a part of the
Free West
I was taught and brought up there, its laws
to abide
And that the land that I live in has God on its side
Oh the history books tell it, they tell it so well

The cavalries charged, the Indians fell
The cavalries charged, the Indians died
For the country was young with God on its side
Oh, the first World War, it came and it went
The reason for fighting, I never could get
But I learned to accept it, accept it with pride
For you don't count the dead when God's on your side
And then the second World War, it came to an end
We forgave the Germans and now we are friends
Though they murdered six million, in the ovens they fried
The Germans now, too, have God on their side

Reverend Murdock was now aware that this song was a slap in the face but was too embarrassed to say anything. He just stared at Howard. A few older men found ways to leave the service by faking an uncontrollable cough. The collection plates continued being passed around, but many refused to contribute. The song continued.

But now we have weapons of chemical dust
And if fire them we're forced to, why then fire them we must
One push of the button and a shot the worldwide
And you never ask questions when God's on your side

The ushers huddled at the rear of the sanctuary. They would not go up to the alter in front of the congregation and thank God for the money they had received, so they headed straight for the church office instead. The song continued.

In many a long hour I've thought on this
That Jesus Christ was betrayed by a kiss
But I can't think for you, you will have to decide
Whether Judas Iscariot had God on his side

The preacher was hanging his head. The congregation
was stirring, but no one knew what to do. Howard was
emotional now, and music was always his best form of
expression. The song concluded.

And now as I leave you, I'm weary as hell
The confusion I'm feelin', there ain't no tongue can tell
The words fill my head and drop to the floor
That if God's on our side, he'll stop the next war.

   ...

Chapter 36
SHOWTIME

The old worn, creaking wooden stairs leading up the poorly lit staircase to the second-floor, Local Draft Board office, reeked of sweat from worried young men like myself who had gone before me for their judgment hearing. Everything about the décor of the building dated back to the forties and fifties. The letters on the green metal textured-glass windowed door spelled "GREENSBURG LOCAL DRAFT BOARD" in standard black block letters.

I WON'T BACK DOWN – Tom Petty

Well, I won't back down
No I won't back down
You could stand me up at the gates of Hell
But I won't back down
No I'll stand my ground
Won't be turned around

And I'll keep this world from draggin' me down
Gonna stand my ground

And I won't back down

Hey baby

There ain't no easy way out (I won't back down)
Hey I will stand my ground
And I won't back down

Well, I know what's right
I got just one life
In a world that keeps on pushin' me around
But I'll stand my ground
And I won't back down

Hey baby
There ain't no easy way out (I won't back down)
Hey I will stand my ground (I won't back down)
And I won't back down

...

I entered, closed the door behind me, and stood there momentarily, taking the surroundings all in and feeling like it would be my last observation before my execution. It was like a step back in time to just after WWII, three or four gray metal chairs thinly padded with green vinyl were placed on a green tiled floor. There was a picture of President Richard Nixon on the plain white wall, dirty marks in various places, and a picture of the American flag flying in the breeze labeled

OUR FLAG - LONG MAY SHE WAVE.

I was on time, but two other boys were ahead of me. One was a farm boy in overalls with a short crew cut. He glanced at me, then returned to resting his head in his hands, his arms propped up with his knees, and staring at his shoes. The other, a biker type with a full scruffy beard and shabby long hair, remained defiant with his arms crossed and an expression on his face of an impending outburst of anger. Since I identified more with the long hair, I chose the empty chair closer to him.

Neither talked, so I finally decided to break the silence and spoke to the long-haired biker.

"Well, what do you think this will be like?"

"I don't give a flying fuck," was his reply.

I figured I better change the subject. "Where are you from?"

"I don't give a flying fuck about that either," was his response. I was dumbfounded, so I said no more. He must have felt guilty or something because he suddenly blurted out, "I was born in Latrobe."

"Oh, really? So was I!" I spoke.

"Can't wait to get the fuck out of there. The only thing good ever came out of Latrobe is Rolling Rock Beer." The negativity was great enough that I was already looking for a way to end the conversation.

"Yeah, that's true," I responded.

"Even that tastes like piss," he replied angrily.

I figured I better keep it lighthearted and change the subject again.

"What year did you graduate from high school?"

"63," he answered.

"So did I!" I replied, and before he could say anything derogatory about the high school ... "What's your name?" I asked.

"Theodore Blanton. But if anybody calls me Theodore, I'll..."

"Teddy? Is that you?" I said excitedly to get him out of his downbeat mood.

I knew him and didn't recognize him under all that hair. I often walked to school with him because I would run into him, passing his house on the way. His family fit in with privileged families on 'The Hill' as we referred to that area of Latrobe. Most families there were wealthy professionals. His dad was a medical doctor and not the only one. Another medical doctor lived beside us.

"Well, fuckin A. Weldon Sipe. The little fairy growed up." What are you doin in this goddam place?"

Because of the angry chip on his shoulder, I let the little fairy remark slide. "The same thing you are, I'm sure."

"Yeah, well, good luck with that," he said. "Where are you hangin' out now? You're not still living around here, are you?"

At that moment, I sure was glad I didn't. "I live in New Mexico."

"What the fuck is in New Mexico?"

Sometimes the plain truth is all you have to explain. "Nothing. Absolutely nothing. That's what I like about it."

"That's cool. I can dig it," was all Teddy could think to add to my answer.

Being apparently a harmless answer, I decided to expand on it. "It's about the only place left that you can turn around 360 degrees and see nothing but your car and the road you drove to get there."

"Cool. New Mexico. Cool," was the only thing he had to say.

"What are you going to do if you lose?"

"Well, I guess they'll just have to kiss my ass," Teddy said emphatically and to the point.

Just then, the door to the boardroom opened, and a buxom woman with a clipboard appeared. Even though only three of us were in the room, and she was only a short distance away, she spoke sharply as though we were quite a way off.

"Mr. Blanton?" She glanced at her list to make sure of Teddy's name. "Theodore Blanton?"

Teddy just sat there motionless. I looked at him, wondering why he wasn't acknowledging her.

She looked at her list again and then, probably because I had glanced at Teddy, zeroed in on him and asked, "Are you Theodore Blanton?"

Teddy slowly stood up but said nothing.

"Mr. Blanton, I believe you're summoned for 1:30?"

Teddy started making some kind of halfhearted and erroneous sign language with his hands and blurted out some gibberish sounding like a deaf person trying to speak.

"You have to speak up. I can't hear you," Teddy mumbled abnormally.

The buxom woman swallowed his act, filled her lungs, and spoke even brasher than before, "I believe you were summoned for 1:30?"

Teddy continued his act as a deaf person. The woman pointed to the clock on the wall, and Teddy acknowledged he knew what she meant. The woman led the way into the boardroom.

Teddy followed but turned back and whispered to me, "It's show time," and proceeded into the boardroom.

As soon as she closed the door behind them, I could hear muffled but sharp words coming from inside. Obviously, Teddy was not there to make any friends.

Sitting there straining to hear what was being said in the boardroom was uncomfortable, so I turned to the farm boy, who continued intently staring at his shoes.

"You can appeal, you know. I am."

He looked up. "What?"

The voices in the boardroom got louder, and the farm boy looked down at his shoes again.

"How old are you?"

He remained looking at his shoes, head in hands. "Nineteen next Christmas. Going on nineteen."

The conversation in the boardroom sounded like things were heating up.

"You can go to Sweden," I said. "Or Canada."

Finally, he spoke, "Don't know nobody there."

The conversation in the boardroom was now boiling over.

"Are you going to try to talk them out of it?" The farm boy's attention went back to his shoes. "Are you a conscientious objector?" I asked.

He looked up. "No, we're farmers, and dad's got a crop of peas almost ready."

The boardroom door flew open. Teddy stomped out in a rage.

"I'll show you motherfuckers!" he bellowed as he headed for the picture of Nixon on the wall, took it off, smashed the glass over the back of a chair, ripped out the picture, and took a bite out of the photo and began chewing on it.

He did not stop there. He proceeded back into the boardroom, spitting his chew on the table in front of the elderly gentleman at the head of the table whom I presumed to be the group's chairman. Coming back out, he suddenly stopped in the doorway, bent over with his ass pointing toward the board members, and left a big fart through an American flag sewn on his pants. I hadn't noticed the flag before.

"You bastard!" the secretary sputtered. The others remained horrorstruck. Although Teddy seemed totally enraged, he looked over at me and suddenly smiled, letting me know that his indignation had all been an act and amusing to him. Finally, he stomped out, slamming the door to the Draft Board Office hard enough to rattle the glass, and I winced for fear the glass would shatter.

All this drama wasn't amusing to the farm boy, who muttered, "Damn Commie."

The secretary managed to regain her composure and came to the door with a clipboard in hand. "Weldon Sipe," she said sternly. "Your next."

My first thought was that there was no chance in hell I would have any success after Teddy's confrontation with the board. Still, I got up and entered the boardroom, and she looked me over with contempt as I started to pass by her.

In a subdued voice, she said, "Now look, young man, we haven't had a conscientious objector in Pennsylvania in more than twenty years, and we're not going to have one now. Understood?"

I kept my composure, unlike Teddy, and silently entered the boardroom. She closed the door behind us.

The boardroom was institutional, looking like the waiting area. The board table was a gray metal base with a gray rubber surface. There were places for six board members. The secretary had a small desk with a stenographer's recorder, some file folders, and another stack of loose papers. She didn't sit at her desk right away but pompously stood beside the older gentleman at the head of the table.

"Sit down, Mr. Sipe," she commanded.

I felt like I was about to be sentenced to the guillotine. But first, I had the privilege of choosing which chair to sit in. Four board members sat at the table, leaving two vacant chairs on one side. I thought my choosing which one to sit in might have some significance as to the outcome, but if it did, it was a mystery to me. I picked the one closest to the chairman, figuring it to appear bold or more aggressive.

"The Chairman of this committee is Sergeant Major Dwight Morehead, U.S. Marine retired. The rest of the four-person board includes Corporal Carl McCloskey, U.S. Marine, retired; Staff Sergeant Thomas Clancy, U.S. Marine, retired; and Thomas Bloomberg, Lieutenant Commander, U.S. Navy retired."

I thought it odd that the Navy Commander was dressed in his uniform. "I am Gertrude Proud, the board's secretary."

Now there's a name I will never forget. Gertrude Proud; a name that couldn't be more fitting. It was on every piece of correspondence that I received from our local draft board, including my draft card. She flipped through a manilla file folder that obviously contained information about me.

"He's been writing us from New Mexico State University, you know, where they recently had those student riots." She referenced the riots trying to associate me with them, which didn't work.

"Oh yes, those student riots," the chairman replied sourly but tactfully as he was handed my file. He reminded me of Mr. Potter in "It's A Wonderful Life." I knew he was a snake in the grass, and I was the grass. Gertrude Proud was standing by with a lawnmower.

There was a clever kind of communication between him and Gertrude that was signified mainly with a glance, a nod, or an inflection in her voice.

"Read Mr. Uh…Sipies…," Morehead started out. "That's Sipe, sir," interrupted Gertrude.

He glanced at the file, "Sipe, OK. If you would please, Gertrude, read just the significant parts of the Selective Service Regulations, would you please."

We all heard what he said, but with the glance between them, he meant to readjust the part he must have quoted many times.

She began reading, "The registrant may…let's see…oh yes, may direct attention to any information in his file which he believes the local board has overlooked or to which he believes it has not given sufficient weight."

"Yes, thank you, Miss Proud," he said then, turning to me, "Now, is there anything that you feel important to add to your file at this time?"

I was boiling over at their dramatic absurdity, "Why do you keep calling it my file? It's yours."

"In a matter of speaking, it is legally yours, although it remains in our possession. We make sure everything we need concerning you is put in it for you."

"Everything I sent you is important," I emphasized. "Is everything in there?"

"I'm sure it is," he said sarcastically, "and we have reviewed it carefully in determining your classification."

After an uncomfortable pause, "So, in requesting this hearing, we assume you have some additional information to add. Is that correct?"

He piously folded his hands on the table as if prepared to listen.

"Well, no. I'm here to protest your decision, I mean, to ask you to reconsider."

I knew when I used the word protest, it was a mistake.

"We have no reason to reconsider anything, young man. In the interest of time, we're not going to bother rehashing old material. Gertrude, what's that part of the law again?"

She had already looked it up, anticipating his asking.

"The members of the local board before whom the registrant appears may place such limitations upon the time in which the registrant may have for his appearance as they deem necessary."

"Yes, that's it. So, in the interest of time, unless you have new information..."

I remembered talking to Reverend Murdock. Hoping that he had done something on my behalf.

"Did Reverend Murdock send a letter?" I blurted out.

Chairman Moorhead looked to Gertrude Proud for the answer.

She was frantically flipping through my file.

"Yes. It's right…here it is."

She handed it to him, and he quickly skimmed through it.

LOOK WHAT THEY'VE DONE TO MY SONG
MA –Melanie

Look what they've done to my song, ma
Look at what they've done to my song
It was the only thing I could do half right
And it's turning out all wrong, ma, look
What they've done to my song

Look what they've done to my brain, ma
Look at what they've done to my brain
Well, they picked it like a chicken bone
And I think that I'm half insane, ma
Look what they've done to my song

Oh, I wish that I could find a good book to live in
Oh, I wish that I could find a good book
Well, if I could find a real good book
I'd never have to come out and look at
What they've done to my song

But maybe, it'll all be all right, ma
Maybe, it'll all be okay
Well, if the people are buying tears
Then I'm gonna be rich some day, ma
Look what they've done to my song

Ils ont changé ma chanson, ma

Ils ont changé ma chanson
C'est la seule chose que je peux faire
Et ce n'est pas bon, ma
Ils ont changé ma chanson

Look what they've done to my song, ma
Look, look what they've done to my song
You know, they tied it up in a plastic bag
And then turned it upside down, oh ma
Look at what they've done to my song

With a smirk, he said, "We should read this one,"

Then he commenced reading it while the song played in the background.

'Dear Sirs: I regret not being able to be present at Weldon Sipe,s hearing. However, it is important to clarify the church,s position regarding conscientious objection. The only religious statement that I am aware of on conscientious objection comes from an article in The Religious Herald, a Baptist magazine from Virginia. They declare that conscientious objection is 'immoral., They say, and I quote, 'The conscientious objector who accepts escape from military service has no part in the noblest national traditions because the history of this nation stands as testimony to the lives of heroes who readily bore arms in mortal combat to win and secure the American heritage of freedom., While this specific pronouncement on conscientious objection is perhaps a little harsh, we in our congregation choose to follow a doctrine of personal choice. We respect the right of each person to arrive at his own convictions. We believe in the principle of freedom of worship and freedom of conscience. We respect the rights of the individual conscience within our fellowship. We have never set up an authoritative creed. Instead, we accept the entire New Testament as our rule of faith and practice, and we seek to lead every member of our fellowship to full comprehension and acceptance of the Spirit of Christ as the guide for all conduct. Since conscientious objection is therefore not based on his church affiliation per se, legal exemption for Weldon from the military would be a privilege granted by the Board in the interest of the civil good. I can attest to Weldon's moral character and lend support to the sincerity of his conviction, rightly or wrongly conceived. He is a lucky, young man that we live in a free country with a just government. Thank you, Reverend James T. Murdock, Jr."

Morehead laid the letter down and piously folded his hands.

"That's a fine letter, don't you agree, Corporal McCloskey?"

McCloskey would have rather been outside, anywhere but there. He was sweating greatly and perhaps feeling claustrophobic. "Yes. Make sure that is in his file," said McCloskey.

"Gertrude, see that this … ", Chairman Morehead added.

Gertrude was already on top of it. "Yes, sir, I certainly will."

"And would you please see that a copy of this letter is put on my desk for all future Christians", Morehead added.

I had to speak up about the letter, "With all due respect, Reverend Murdock doesn't speak for all Christians!"

Clancy was sitting there like a weasel and not participating any more than he had to.

"That may be so, Mr. Sipe," Clancy said, jumping in at last. "But take the Catholics, for instance. The Roman Catholic Church is the largest single religious group in America. Rank-and-file Catholics are very loyal and very patriotic. They would never question American policy in Vietnam, or anywhere else for that matter."

"I believe that," I said. "That's why they still have a Pope!" After a few moments, I added, "What about Methodists. They denounce war and recognize the right to conscientious objection."

"I'm a Methodist," Jones chimed in. "I don't know what you're talking about, but during the Civil War, Lincoln said the Methodist Episcopal Church sent more soldiers to the field, more nurses to the hospitals, and more prayers to heaven than ...."

"You're not a Methodist, are you, Weldon?" Morehead brought the focus back on point.

"No," I said emphatically.

"Then, in the interest of time, we must move on."

Clancy sat there irritated. "Do you know what we did to Conscientious Objectors during World War II?"

I wasn't sure that he was old enough to have fought in World War II, so I didn't give any response.

"We put them in stockades and starved them to see how long our boys could last in German concentration camps."

I glanced around. It appeared to me that we all thought that Clancy had mentally checked out.

Morehead focused the group again. "Are you married, Weldon?"

It took me a moment to recover from Clancy and catch up with the Chairman. "Well…yes."

"What does your wife have to say about all this?" He asked. "We're kind of apart right now."

"You mean you're separated?" he asked, and I assumed he would now plan another attack.

"Yes."

"I'm sorry to hear that," he responded sarcastically. "Did your feelings about the military have anything to do with your separation?"

I came to the realization that I, like Teddy, was not going to win anything at this hearing. I looked at each of them as they were perched for the kill. My thoughts went back to how Teddy responded, and I decided to imitate him.

"I don't give a flying fuck," I shouted as I stood up.

They were all shocked. I could tell that Clancy was confused by the look on his face.

"Are you one of those hippies that believe in free love?" Clancy asked.

He seemed to have lost it, but he wouldn't be ignored. "How many times a week do you have sex? Once? Twice?"

We were all shocked. I choked; Gertrude stopped typing. Morehead tried to ignore him.

"Your application for conscientious objection is a personal matter too, Weldon. We're just trying to understand the extent of your sincerity."

He motioned me to sit down. Hesitantly, I did.

Lieutenant Commander Bloomberg had been looking through my file and found something disturbing to him. "How could you take money for making submarines and still call yourself a pacifist?"

The sex questions were embarrassing, but I feared this question most of all. I had no prepared answer, but some words came to me.

"I was afraid to say I believed in peace! I was afraid I'd lose my job! I was afraid to say I was a CO even after discovering I was a CO!"

My answer wasn't compelling, but the Navy Commander seemed pleased with it. He nodded that he understood. Maybe he agreed with me. I don't know. I'll never know.

Clancy was still attacking me.

"How do we know that you aren't just trying to get out of the service. Are you afraid, Weldon? Is that it? You're a coward?"

I was caught off guard.

"No, I'm not a coward. I tried to enlist once when I was in high school."

I knew I shouldn't have said that, and the Chairman wasn't going to let that go by.

"You tried to enlist!" the chairman questioned.

"Yes," I replied, realizing this might have cost me a favorable outcome. Now I had no choice but to give enough details of what happened in a way that would support my claim to being a conscientious objector. I resorted to using material I had written in my practice thesis.

"I went to the local recruiter's office in Latrobe. It was in 1963, after I had graduated from high school. It was raining, and it was a small office lined with army-green filing cabinets. I remember there was a large American flag and a US Army one as well."

"Spare us the graphic details and just get to the point," barked the Chairman.

"I can't. The details set the foundation for your understanding of why I would go to the recruiter's office in the first place."

So, I continued with my narrative.

"At first, I saw only the top of Sergeant Snaps' head and his nameplate on his desk. He was turned away from me and facing the window watching the rain outside. A cloud of smoke radiated into the air from his unseen figure, and I believe he was smoking pot!"

I looked around the boardroom. Mentioning smoking pot got their undivided attention, so I continued with my narrative and kept pot included.

"I walked slowly and quietly toward the Sergeant's desk, not wanting to startle him. The Sergeant's desk had several personal momentums of his tour in Vietnam: some metals but mostly pictures of his comradery with various Vietnamese girls. Because of my inexperience, the gallery of pictures of pretty girls gave me much reason to discredit the character of the recruiter. Our conversation went something like this."

"Excuse me, Sir?" I spoke in a subdued voice, not to startle the Sergeant.

He twirled around and hastily snuffed out his half-smoked joint by squeezing the hot end with his bare fingers!

"Sorry, I didn't hear you come in," he said as he stuffed the remains of the joint in his uniform shirt pocket. I assumed he was saving it for later.

His uniform looked worn, as if his better days of military service were behind him. It seemed he really hadn't much to do. His desk was very bare and orderly.

"It's not like they're standing in line to sign up these days," he grumbled.

Then he folded his hands on the desk and asked what he could do for me? I went right to the point by stating that I wanted to enlist.

He snapped back, "Well, that's good 'cause I'm not selling girl scout cookies."

"Are you eighteen?" he asked me as he fumbled through a stack of application forms in a manilla folder on his desk.

"Yes. Last April," I told him.

"Well, okay then," he responded as he started filling out a form, even though it was obvious he was feeling anxious, probably from the effects of the marijuana. "What branch of the service do you want? I'm an Army Recruiter, but I can get you into …."

"It doesn't matter," I said.

I knew it was the wrong thing to say by the expression on his face. He stopped writing and tried to look me squarely in the eyes, but he couldn't focus.

"What the … what kind a job are you looking to do?"

I didn't answer quickly, so he blurted out some options. "Paratrooper, infantry, medical corps … ?"

"Medical corp. I want to be a medic," I said.

"Alright. OK, Medical Corp," he hesitantly replied.

I stopped with my narration and looked around the boardroom. They were all spellbound, and I knew I had to have a great finish. What was best to tell them was the truth, and I did.

I interrupted Sergeant Snap while he was filling out the paper. "I have some conditions."

He sat back in his chair and folded his arms. "What conditions?"

"I don't want to carry a gun."

I paused again to gauge the local board members' reaction. Their expressions varied, and not all expressed contempt.

I told them that Snap, however, didn't flinch.
"I see," he said. "Anything else?"

"I don't want to wear a uniform," I said as my second condition, then added, "Not a military uniform anyway. I want to wear white, with big red crosses on my front and back. I want everyone to see that I am a medic, not a soldier."

By his red face, it seemed Snap's blood was beginning to boil.

I paused again to gauge the response to my constraints, and I could tell some of the board members were also at their boiling point. I continued.

"Anything else?" asked Sergeant Snap.

"Yes," I said. Then as my finale, "I want the right to help anyone wounded, whether man or woman or a child, whether enemy or foe."

The jaws of most of the board members dropped. I paused so what I had just told them would sink in.

"The next thing I knew," I told the board members, "I was flying out the door of the recruiter's office and sliding on my ass on the rainy, slippery sidewalk."

The unempathetic recruiter shouted, "I'm not going to sign your smart ass up to go kill yourself," as he slammed the door in my face.

This ended my dialogue with the board.

As I left, the board members' reactions varied and changed from second to second. I had stated my case as best I could. I didn't expect to win, but hopefully, I made it as difficult for them to deny my request.

I was distraught when I reached the bottom of the stairs and entered the street after leaving the Draft Board hearing. I took a breath and leaned against the side of the building, trying to regain my composure. It was a humiliating experience. Things would never be the same, and perhaps I had a feeling of what was to follow.

I was teary-eyed as I recalled what Gertrude Proud said when I first walked in, "Now look, young man, we haven't had a conscientious objector in Pennsylvania in more than twenty years, and we're not going to have one now. Understood?"

She knew how it was going to end and had told me so.

DON'T BOGART THAT JOINT – Fraternity of Man, Elliot Ingbar and Larry Wagner

Don't Bogart that joint, my friend
Pass it over to me
Don't Bogart that joint, my friend
Pass it over to me

Roll another one
Just like the other one
You've been hangin' onto it
And I sure would like a hit

Don't Bogart that joint, my friend
Pass it over to me
Don't Bogart that joint, my friend
Pass it over to me

Rooooooooll another one
Just like the other one
That one's burned just 'bout to the end
So comon and be a real friend

Don't Bogart that joint, my friend
Pass it over to me

Don't Bogart that joint, my friend
Pass it over to me

Well, I had stood up to the draft, one of the most courageous moments in my life. Unofficially, they told me that my file would be reviewed again. Still, it was unlikely that my classification would be changed. Now it was my choice: five years in prison or the rest of my life in Canada.

A very long fancy Harley was parked illegally on the street in front of me. It was very unique. Teddy came out of nowhere. He must have been hanging around waiting for me. In one quick swoop, he pulled out a partially exposed parking ticket that a traffic cop had tucked under the edge of his bike seat. He tossed it into the street without even bothering to look at it. Then, Teddy leaned against the building alongside me. I wiped my eyes with the back of my hands.

"You just gotta know when things are fucked up," he said. "You know what I mean?"

I didn't answer. Teddy pulled a joint from his shirt pocket and lit it up. He toked on it until the end of the joint glowed bright red, inhaled deeply, and held it in until he needed fresh air.

"And things are really fucked up," he added.

He extended the joint to me. I fumbled with it and immediately started coughing after inhaling the first toke. I had smoked many times, but this was a stronger pot than anything I had before.

"Are you going to appeal their decision?" He asked.

"I can't appeal unless one of the board members votes to grant me the CO classification," I said. "I don't think that's going to happen."

"So, tell me about New Mexico," said Teddy.

We stayed there on that city street, at the top of the hill, talking for a while.

A few days later, I got a letter that I was officially denied the Conscientious Objector classification. There was a factual error on the notice. The notice stated that the voting tally was unanimous for the denial by 3 to 0. But there were four board members in attendance! After some thought, I concluded that the Navy guy, Lieutenant Commander Thomas Bloomberg, must have supported me. Gertrude Proud must have exercised her secretarial power and erased all records that Bloomberg ever attended the hearing. This meant I was not eligible to further appeal the board's decision because it was unanimous according to the erroneous notice.

Chapter 37

THE VERDICT IS IN

I called the Central Committee for Conscientious Objectors and informed them of all that had happened, including the questions and my responses to them as they had asked me to do. Bob Seeley wrote everything down.

"What do I do now?" I asked.

"What do you want to do?" He asked.

"Well," I replied. "My only choices are to go to prison or Canada, and right now, I am leaning toward Canada."

"Don't do that!" he said sharply. "It's not time for that. Just sit tight for now and let me get back to you. In the meantime, write down what you just told me and make two copies. Get one copy into your file, drive it to the Local Board today, and watch them put it in your file personally. Then send the other copy to me in case they accidentally lose it."

It wasn't but a couple of hours after going to the local board that I got a phone call from a lawyer for the ACLU.

Since the ACLU wasn't mentioned in the handbook by the Central Committee, I asked, "What is the ACLU?"

"The American Civil Liberties Union is a group of Lawyers that work to defend and preserve the individual rights and liberties guaranteed to every person in this country by the Constitution. We provide free legal assistance in cases of individuals whose liberties are at risk."

"How do you know about me?" I asked,

"You have been communicating with Bob Seeley of the Central Committee for Conscientious Objectors, right?"

"Yes."

"Well, from his notes, he informed us of your situation, and we said we would like to look further into your case. We need your permission to do that."

"What exactly can you do for me?"

"That depends on your intentions," the lawyer said,

"I am intending to go to Canada. That beats going to prison, I think."

"If you have decided already to go to Canada, then we can't help you. But if you stay, we will review your file in detail, and if there is enough evidence to make a case, we will represent you in court if the Local Board wants to fight us. We will seek to have your draft notice rescinded."

"Let me understand you clearly. You will represent me in trying to overturn my being drafted?"

"Yes."

"If you win, I am free?"

"Yes."

"But if you lose, I go to jail?"

"Well...yes."

"Why would I take a chance on you guys when I can go to Canada now for certain freedom?"

"You know that under the current laws, you can never return to the US?"

"Yes."

"Ever! Again! Not even for a visit or a funeral!"

I do not remember getting any sleep that night. I never considered living in Canada -- always figuring that I was born an American, would live as an American, and would die as an American. But now I had to decide my life's outcome.

The same attorney called again the following day as planned. I really hadn't made my mind up.

"I feel like my country has abandoned me," I said to him.

"Look, about your considering going to Canada," he said. "Just imagine all the war resisters that you leave behind if you go to Canada. If you can't follow your convictions, then how will they?"

He was partially right, of course. This was a far greater concern than me avoiding the draft. How could I live with myself if I just left? On the other hand, if I stayed and ended up in jail, what kind of life would I have after serving prison time? I could imagine many doors of opportunity would be closed to me. On the other hand, I would surely be free in Canada. There was no draft Canada. Enlistment is voluntary.

However, after much soul-searching, I chose the ACLU.

"We paid a visit to your Local Board yesterday," were the ACLU's lawyer's first words telling me what happened. "We asked to see your file. The Secretary was reluctant but realized anything she said would be held against her. She gave in. We already knew what was in your file, of course, but we pretended it was all new to us. There is ample evidence for a case that your civil rights have been violated, so we handed it back to her and told her we would see her in court. The word fear comes to mind describing the expression on her face. We abruptly left without saying another word. The ball is in her court, and we'll see how it plays out."

A day later, I got a letter from the Local Draft Board. It said, "This is to inform you that your draft notice was sent in error. Please disregard the notice."

Now I knew that the ACLU's plan worked. The Local Board didn't want the embarrassment of a hearing and the publicity it would initiate.

I wasn't being forced to go to Canada, but I had no reason to stay in Pennsylvania. The poor economy would limit my job prospects, and being labeled a draft dodger certainly would not help either. My family practically disowned me, and I had no friends around anymore. So, let's see: no job, friends, or family. It was time to leave and start again.

I gave my mother the keys to my VW and told her in a note to sell it if she didn't want it. She was too proud to ever accept money, so this way, she would feel that she earned it for putting up with me. I didn't tell her that it was a parting gift as I was leaving the country for good.

Now, I could start anew with the letter from Jutsie of the War Resisters League, offering to be my sponsor and employer. Like most others involved in the Anti-Draft program, Jutsie assumed that my opposition to the war in Vietnam stemmed from principle. As such, I was likely to become an outstanding citizen. Although all Canadians didn't share this opinion, the government made no attempt to integrate different cultures. As a result, an atmosphere of freedom prevails. The Canadian Government has never launched a war and seldom becomes involved in one directly.

I called the number on Jutsie's letterhead. It was a warm, friendly conversation, and she had a sweet, laid-back voice. We agreed on a day and time to meet at the Niagara Falls border crossing.

Chapter 38
A LITTLE HELP FROM OUR FRIENDS

I could walk to the house where Teddy grew up, which I did. Teddy was there and some of his motorcycle gang and they agreed to take me to the Canadian border.

Our assembled motorcycle gang, which included about 12 cycles, headed out late that afternoon. I road with Teddy. We could not make much headway because of a slow-moving caravan of "Good Sam Club" motor homes and campers heading north toward Canada. Teddy tried several times to pass a motor home on the curvy road. Still, we encountered oncoming traffic every time. The others in the gang were having the same problem.

From what I could see, retirees were driving a convoy of motorhomes in front of our motorcycles. They were vacationers taking their time, refusing to be hassled by our motorcycle gang. It's not that they were trying to keep control of the road and were courteous but trying to stay together. One driver stuck his arm out and waved us on, but more oncoming traffic forced us back when we tried to pass. When the caravan began to climb a long upward grade, the caravan slowed to a crawl. Teddy decided to stay behind the caravan after failing to pass several times, and the others followed suit. Suddenly Teddy started singing America the Beautiful!

Oh, beautiful for spacious skies for amber waves of grain
For purple mountain majesties above the fruited plain!"

The other bikers decided to join in the singing!

America! America! God shed his grace on thee
And crown thy good with brotherhood from sea to shining
sea.

The whole gang was singing. In fact, as the song progressed, not only was the whole motorcycle gang singing, but people in the caravan joined in too! Soon it sounded like a large choir.

Oh, beautiful for pilgrim feet whose stern, impassioned
stress
A thorough fare of freedom beat across the wilderness!

America! America! God mend thine every flaw
Confirm thy soul in self-control thy liberty in law."

Finally, the road grade went downward for a long distance, and we were able to pass. The singing continued.

Oh, beautiful for patriot dream that sees beyond the years
Thine alabaster cities gleam undimmed by human tears!

An old couple was singing as Teddy, and I passed by. Teddy held up his arm and gave them the peace sign. They reciprocated.

America! America!
God shed his grace on thee
And crown thy good with brotherhood from sea to shining
sea.

Chapter 39
CAMPFIRE REFLECTIONS

My butt and leg muscles were sore from sitting behind Teddy. We camped for the night in a state park somewhere in Upstate New York, and I figured we would make it to the Canadian border in an hour or so.

We had a small campfire going, and Teddy toked up on the biggest joint I had ever seen, and it looked like a backwoods cigar rather than a joint. He passed it to me, and I took a hit and immediately sounded half-choked when I tried to add to our conversation about our day's travel.

"It's all one country, you know."

"Fuckin A man," responded Teddy. "Great nature, nice little towns, and nice people, well, except for the militaristic political assholes smearing the country's face in shit." When Teddy had something nice to say, he always followed it with something negative.

"Answer me one question," I asked to break his negativity. "Why are so many people so whole-heartedly committed to obeying authority?"

Teddy took another toke. "Don't understand," he said. "And I don't care to at this moment in my life."

I continued my thought. "Why are people willing to lose everything, their lives, their families, their fortunes to win a war, but they aren't willing to sacrifice one thing, to fight for peace or their families."

"I'll never commit to any slime-ball authority, especially when they imprison resistors and shoot college kids."

"Fuckin A, man," I responded in Teddy's vernacular.
He liked that and responded with a little smile.

"Fuckin A!"

Chapter 40
THE CURTAIN FALLS

We arrived at the Canadian border and stopped about a hundred yards from the border station. I got off the cycle and stood there.

Peace Train - Cat Stevens

Now I've been happy lately
Thinking about the good things to come
And I believe it could be
Something good has begun
Oh, I've been smiling lately
Dreaming about the world as one
And I believe it could be
Someday it's going to come
'Cause out on the edge of darkness
There rides the peace train
Oh, peace train take this country
Come take me home again
Now I've been smiling lately
Thinkin' about the good things to come
And I believe it could be
Something good has begun
Oh, peace train sounding louder
Glide on the peace train
Ooh-ah, ee-ah, ooh-ah
Come on now, peace train
Yes, peace train holy roller
Everyone jump upon the peace train
Ooh-ah, ee-ah, ooh-ah

Come on now, peace train
Get your bags together
Go bring your good friends too
Because it's getting nearer
It soon will be with you
Now come and join the living
It's not so far from you
And it's getting nearer
Soon it will all be true
Oh, peace train sounding louder
Glide on the peace train
Ooh-ah, ee-ah, ooh-ah
Come on now peace train
Peace train
Now I've been crying lately
Thinkin' about the world as it is
Why must we go on hating?
Why can't we live in bliss?
'Cause out on the edge of darkness
There rides a peace train
Oh, peace train take this country
Come take me home again

...

Finally, my journey ended, or should I say my new life was just beginning. I was financially broke except for the few hundred dollars I had kept to file for landed immigrant status as a Canadian citizen. On the Canadian side, a hippie-decorated VW bus was just beyond the border station. Jutsie stepped out of it and looked toward me, giving me a peace sign and walking into the border station building.

"You sure?" I asked Teddy. "It's a real brotherhood, like what my old Prof used to say would be a 'beloved community.'"

"No," said Teddy. "I was born here in the US of A, and they'll just have to like it or kiss my ass."

He extended his hand, and I shook it. "Each his own way. At least they won't have ME to kick around anymore."

"Fuckin A, man," he replied. "Good luck."

"Thanks. You, too, Ted. You'll need it. You can come to see the alabaster cities gleaming any time you want."

The gang started their cycles and made a U-turn. As they headed out, Teddy raised a peace sign high in the air, and I did the same. Over the roar of the cycling noise, I shouted, "Something good has begun."

Even though the circumstances at that time and not by choice made Canada my haven, I remembered that in her letter to me, Jutsie had said to bring 300 dollars in cash and declare that I wished to obtain landed immigrant status, one of three ways to enter Canada. As a tourist or a student are two other ways to obtain entrance.

I was nervous because of my experiences crossing the border into Mexico from El Paso on routine Tequila runs while a student at New Mexico State.

One time, the U.S. Immigration officer asked in what state I was born.

I wasn't listening carefully and answered, "U.S.A.," to which he barked, "I didn't ask what country, and I asked what state." He was looking at my paper bag containing several bottles of Tequila. The look of repulsion on his face was a wake-up call. "If you're going to be a smart ass, I can detain you for three days."

"Pennsylvania," I hurriedly replied. He waved me on.

I hoped the Canadian border patrol wasn't like the ones between Mexico and the U.S. Jutsie met me just inside the entrance door and immediately gave some advice. "Answer their questions honestly. Avoid politics about your coming here to avoid the draft."

"Why are they ..."

"They don't care. They use an application form, and your answers are evaluated by a point system. I will help you as I am your sponsor and your employer."

As soon as I entered, it was evident that immigrants were welcomed.

I completed all the business of getting through customs, thanks to Jutsie. Since I walked in with just the clothes on my back, it was a simple affair. The $300 in cash I would use for the following semester's graduate school tuition covered the fee to immediately apply for citizenship and served as adequate proof that I was not penniless. Jutsie spoke up and vouched for me when asked if I had employment.

"Come on," said Jutsie as we walked from the border station. "I'll introduce you to some of the gang here who've already come over."

It suddenly hit me that I was walking on Canadian soil, not as a foreigner, but as a citizen. I was enthusiastic to begin anew. We climbed into her battered VW van painted with bright-colored flowers and peace symbols to hide some dents and rust spots. The door squeaked and was difficult to close, and the lock finally engaged on my second try.

Her VW was a befitting vehicle, and Jutsie seemed akin to it. She also looked worn at first glance, plain with very little make-up, but still under her flower child pretense, quite naturally attractive.

"Don't forget, you're in a new country now," she said to break the silence.

Every time she spoke, there was a welcoming warmth in her voice, a politeness that drew me instantly to her. I noticed an occasional French-Canadian accent when she first spoke at the inspection station. I was not expecting a foreign accent, but I had to remind myself I was the foreigner this time.

She seemed to know my thoughts, including my natural uneasiness toward being a newcomer. I looked through my open passenger window at the border station as we drove away. All the things I had worked for all my life were gone, and now I was starting over.

I looked toward Horseshoe Falls, and I remembered that there was one more thing I had to do.

"Would you mind if we stopped at the falls," I asked.

We parked in a parking lot and walked to a lookout point closest to the water. I leaned over the railing to see the water making its final way to the top edge of the falls just a few yards away.

"You're not going to do anything stupid, are you?" asked Jutsie.

"No," I responded as I took out my draft card. "I wasn't draft dodging," I said. "I didn't burn the flag. And I didn't illegally come to Canada. I walked to Canada on my own accord."

I couldn't think of anything more to say as I reminded myself and her that I wasn't a fugitive.

Jutsie looked over at me, wondering what I was thinking and feeling. "You don't have any regrets, do you?" she said.

"Of course, I have regrets, doesn't everybody? But I can live with mine. I can't speak for others and the choices they're still making concerning the draft and the war."

I finally let go of my draft card. Even though the current was swift, it took a while for the card to gain momentum and move away from the slower waters next to the shore.

We both leaned against the railing and watched it make its way toward the edge, intermittently hitting several protruding rocks along the way. It gradually worked its way free to continue its journey to the drop.

GOLDEN SLUMBERS / CARRY THAT WEIGHT –

The Beatles

Once there was a way
To get back homeward
Once there was a way
To get back home
Sleep, pretty darling
Do not cry
And I will sing a lullaby
Golden slumbers fill your eyes
Smiles awake when you rise
Sleep, pretty darling
Do not cry
And I will sing a lullaby
Once there was a way
To get back homeward
Once there was a way
To get back home
Sleep, pretty darling
Do not cry
And I will sing a lullaby
Boy, you gonna carry that weight
Carry that weight
A long time
Boy...

   ...

It finally reached the edge where it hesitated as if to be still considering the consequences. "I may not have done what I was supposed to, but I did what was right," I said as it disappeared over the falls.

My mind was racing with thoughts. I thought about the many different choices that all of us from the '60s made. No matter what each of us did, whatever road we decided to travel, the common thread that bound us together was the music of those times. The music was also used in the protesting, in the battlefields, and probably in the prisons. It was a reflection of us, and it gave us purpose and meaning.

"I'll miss the music," I blurted out.

She chuckled. "We have Rock and Roll!" She knew what I meant. It was not that I missed it now or was afraid Canadians didn't listen to the same music. It was that I knew that, like everything else, our youth, the protests, the consequences of our actions, our music would someday fade away into rewritten history.

Chapter 41
NEVER MISTAKE THE SILENCE

LOOKING FOR AN ECHO – Kenny Vance and the Planotones

At Erasmus Hall High School, we used to harmonize
Me and Benny and Ira and two Italian guys
We were singing oldies, but they were newies then
And today when I play my own 45's, I remember when…

We'd practice in a subway, in a lobby or a hall
Crowded in a doorway, singing doo wops to the wall
And if we went to a party and they wouldn't let us sing
We'd lock ourselves in the bathroom, and nobody could get in

'Cause we were looking for an echo, an answer to our sond
A place to be in harmony
A place we almost found

And the girls would gather 'round us, and our heads would really swell
We'd sing songs by the Moonglows, the Harptones, and the Dells
And when we sang "Sincerely," we really sang it high
Even though it was falsetto, we almost reached the sky

269

We've sung a lot of changes since 1955
And a lot of bad arrangements we've tried to harmonize
Now we've turned into oldies, but we were newies then
And today when I play my own 45's, I remember when…

We were looking for an echo, an answer to our sound
A place to be in harmony
A place we almost found

...

The '60s are long gone but never mistake the silence over the years gone by as acceptance of things as they are.

An unexplainable feeling hit me when I realized my ultimate act of defiance was complete. I had stood up for what I believed in and was willing to take the consequences for doing so. My fight against the draft was finally over, and I was starting over in Canada.

Freedom of dissent, at whatever the cost, is the basic ingredient for freedom in both Canada and the United States. Sometime in our past, Americans have begun to overlook this, or at least some have attempted to redefine what freedom means.

I have no regrets, but I have had to come to grips with the realization that the things I wanted to see didn't happen with all the years that have gone by.

The End

www.ingramcontent.com/pod-product-compliance
Lightning Source LLC
Chambersburg PA
CBHW071411300726

48976CB00006B/2063